Cry of the Giraffe

CRY OF THE GIRAFFE

BASED ON A TRUE STORY

JUDIE ORON

Edited by Barbara Berson
Interior designed by Monica Charny
Cover designed by Sheryl Shapiro

Annick Press Ltd.

We acknowledge the support of the Canada Council for the Arts, the Ontario Arts Council, and the Government of Canada through the Canada Book Fund (CBF) for our publishing activities.

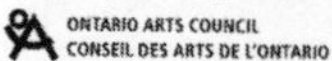

Cataloging in Publication

Oron, Judie

Cry of the giraffe : based on a true story / Judie Oron.

ISBN 978-1-55451-271-3 (pbk.).—ISBN 978-1-55451-272-0 (bound)

1. Jews—Ethiopia—Juvenile fiction. I. Title.

PS8629.R56C79 2010 C813'.6 C2010-903147-4

Printed in Canada.

Mixed Sources
Product group from well-managed forests, controlled sources and recycled wood or fiber
www.fsc.org Cert no. SW-COC-002358
© 1996 Forest Stewardship Council

Annick Press is committed to protecting our natural environment. As part of our efforts, this book is printed on 100% post-consumer recycled fibers.

Published in the U.S.A. by
Annick Press (U.S.) Ltd.

Distributed in Canada by
Firefly Books Ltd.
66 Leek Crescent
Richmond Hill, ON
L4B 1H1

Distributed in the U.S.A. by
Firefly Books (U.S.) Inc.
P.O. Box 1338
Ellicott Station
Buffalo, NY 14205

Visit our website at www.annickpress.com

Front cover images: woman © iStockphoto Inc./Klaas Lingbeek-van Kranen; background © Melinda Nagy/Dreamstime.com. Back cover image: © Judie Oron

In memory of my parents—Ilene, z'l, who taught me about mothering; and Charlie, z'l, who showed me the importance of storytelling. —J.O.

Map of Africa and Surrounding Area

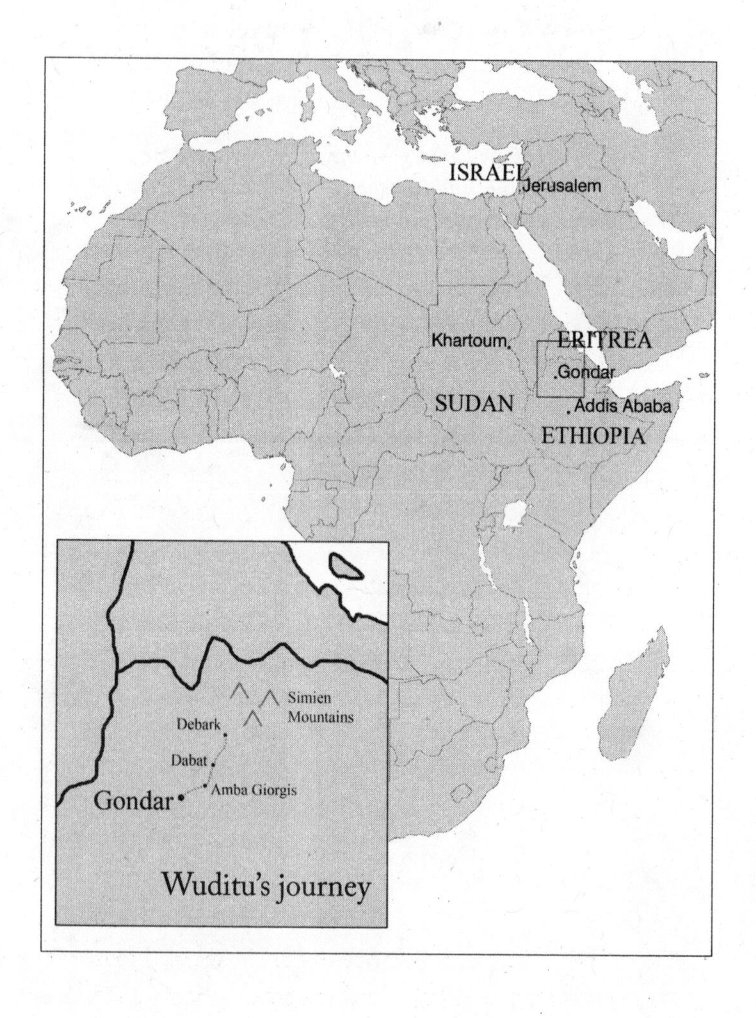

Note to Readers

Slavery! Captivity! The words bring to mind the transport of human beings from the African continent to the New World. That happened a long time ago. But today, in many countries, people are still being held captive, whether by other people or by circumstances. Wuditu's account is an example of how this can and does happen to children in Ethiopia. But the difference between their lives and those of children in other parts of the world is merely circumstantial.

Historical sources tell us that a group of Jews fled southward into Egypt more than 2000 years ago, after the destruction of the First Temple in Jerusalem. Three hundred years later, when their security was again threatened, a later generation followed the Nile River into Ethiopia. There, they established a Jewish kingdom, alongside the people already living there. Jewish kings and queens ruled the area for hundreds of years, fought battles, and were triumphant over the local tribes who wanted to subdue them.

In the seventeenth century, a coalition of forces defeated the Jewish kingdom. Many Jews were slaughtered, some were forced to convert to Christianity, and those that survived and did not convert fled to Ethiopia's remote highlands, where they practiced their religion with great strictness, believing that they were the last surviving Jews in the world.

The Jews, who called themselves Beta Israel, or "House of Israel," rebuilt their villages and eked out a bare existence under new harsh laws that reflected the fact that they h for centuries been a hated enemy. They had become *falashas*, meaning strangers, a people who were now forbidden to own land.

Forced to pay rent to local landowners, the Beta Israel subsidized their farming livelihood by selling their crafts—iron tools, woven cloth, and pottery. Because they used fire in their iron and pottery work, they came afoul of their Christian neighbors, who, like other tribes in Africa, believed that those who worked with fire had made a pact with evil spirits. They believed that the Beta Israel could cast spells with a mere glance or turn themselves into hyenas that "ate" (that is, killed) humans. Jews were often accused of causing the destruction of their neighbors' crops or even of bringing about their illness and death. They were sometimes banished from their villages and forced to rebuild in more remote areas.

When Israel gained independence in 1948, Ethiopian Jews waited to be reunited with their brethren in the Holy Land. Sadly, this took several decades to come to fruition. In the 1970s the way was paved in Israel for the community to fulfill their dream, but a Marxist dictator, Mengistu Haile Mariam, refused to allow them to leave Ethiopia.

Israel sent emissaries to the Beta Israel villages, instructing them to trek several hundred kilometers through rugged territory infested with bandits and warring armies to neighboring Sudan, an Arab state that was a declared enemy of Israel.

The Jews were told to pretend to be refugees, fleeing from Ethiopia because of famine and the brutal war between Ethiopia's Marxist forces and the rebels who years later would succeed in overthrowing the regime. The plan was for the Beta Israel to hide in the refugee camps, which sheltered thousands of people escaping the country's harsh conditions. There, in the camps, they waited—sometimes for months and even years—to be taken to Israel.

Israel sent covert agents to Sudan to seek out the Beta Israel and try to provide them with some protection from the ongoing hunger, lawlessness, and diseases of the camps. Whenever circumstances allowed, the agents led them to a remote place in the desert, where planes landed on secret makeshift runways. Within seconds after landing, teams of commandos rushed out and quickly herded the starving and destitute Beta Israel onto planes with interiors that had been emptied of seats in order to accommodate hundreds of people. Within minutes, the planes took off for Israel. Doctors treated the sick en route and babies were born onboard. Those agents who remained behind hurried to erase all evidence that a plane had landed illegally in Sudan.

More than 4000 Ethiopian Jews died, either on the journey or in the refugee camps waiting to be flown to Israel. Wuditu and Lewteh are two of the thousands who tried but failed to reach Israel by this route.

Today, there are approximately 120,000 Ethiopian Jews living in Israel, and every year thousands of them converge on Jerusalem to honor those who died on their way to the Holy Land.

Wuditu's Family Tree

Tarik (Wuditu's deceased grandmother)
Rahel (Wuditu's mother) married Berihun (Wuditu's father), who then married Melkeh (Lewteh's mother)
Dawid (Wuditu's brother by Rahel)
Wubalu, Aster, Lewteh, Mulu'alem (Wuditu's stepsisters by Melkeh, in order of their ages)

Wuditu's Cousins/Uncles

(in order of appearance)

Cousin Daniel
Cousin Melessa
Uncle Alemu
Cousin Maru (Daniel's son)
Uncle Yonah (in Gojjam)

Other Characters

(in order of appearance)

Kes Sahalu (the *kes* [rabbi] in Dibebehar)
Yosef (the teacher in Dibebehar)
Hailu (the girl from school)
Waga (the man sent to help the refugees in Tikil Dingay)
Kes Baruch (the *kes* in Senvetige)
Berreh (the hotel owner)
Elias (the teacher in Amba Giorgis)
The *meloxie* (the holy woman in Amba Giorgis)
Yelemwork (the holy woman's granddaughter)

Prologue

Every year on February 21, I phone her. And every time, I ask her the same question: "Why are we still alive?"

No matter how many times I ask, her answer is always the same: "Because there was a wind."

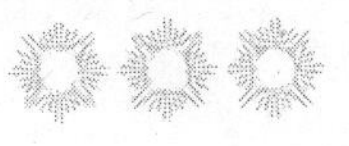

My name is Wuditu. When I was 13, my father took our family from our Ethiopian village to another country, Sudan. From there, we hoped to get to a place we called Yerusalem. While we were in Sudan, my little sister Lewteh and I were taken from our family. Not too long after that, I had to leave my sister. At the time, I thought it was the only way to save her. I was wrong, and my life was changed forever.

But I don't want to start my story there. I'll begin instead before that, when I was still a child in my village. I was nine years old, and it was Fasika, the Passover holiday for my people. We call ourselves the Beta Israel, which means the House of Israel in our language, Amharic. Hundreds of years ago, a foreign army came to Yerusalem. They defeated our people and destroyed our Holy Temple. After that, our ancestors fled our ancient homeland and followed the Nile River into Ethiopia. They settled in the highlands, where we have lived ever since. But even though our bodies are here in Ethiopia, our hearts have always longed to go home. This is where my story begins.

Part One

The Village

Chapter 1

Dibebehar, 1985

Wuditu, 9, and Lewteh, 6

"Aiee! Lewteh, what are you doing?" I called, my voice cracking with nervous excitement.

In only a few hours it would be dark, the first night of Fasika, and all through the last weeks we'd been rushing to get everything ready. Our men had woven the cloth for everyone's new clothes. All our earthenware pots had been thrown away and our women had made a whole new set. Even the baskets we used for serving our meals were thrown away and new ones woven specially for the feast. Our Christian neighbors had come by to wish us a good holiday and to assure us that our animals and pastures would be well looked after during the eight days that we rested. Soon, everything would be ready!

We do all this to remember that in ancient times our people were slaves in Egypt. A great leader named Moses helped us to escape and led us to freedom in the land we call Yerusalem.

Since then, every year at Fasika we celebrate the fact that our forefathers were delivered from slavery. They were in such a hurry to leave that they couldn't wait for their bread to rise. They had only flat, unleavened bread to eat and so, on Passover, we do the same.

This morning, we'd swept our houses clean and burnt all the leftover leaven, and for the whole eight days of Fasika we would be eating only flat bread, called *kitta*. It doesn't taste very good. But that's all right. It's important to remember these things.

"Lewteh!" I called again. There was still so much to do before nightfall. "Where is that girl? It's just like her to disappear right about now!"

Of all my sisters, it was Lewteh whom I loved the most. When she was little, I pretended that she was my baby. I carried her around on my back in a special pouch called an *ankalba*. From the moment she began to walk, she followed me everywhere on fat little legs. Now that she was older, though, she had become such a troublemaker! Where I was responsible, and a bit timid, she was always getting into trouble, and I was usually the one getting her out of it. Who knows what she'd gotten into now?

After searching everywhere for her, I ran around to the back of the house, where my mother had put all our discarded cooking pots. And there was Lewteh—sweet, tiny, her eyes sparkling with excitement—surrounded by a mess of broken plates, holding an impressively large pot high over her head and practically teetering under its weight. Then I watched, speechless, as she hurled the pot, nearly knocking herself over in the process.

"Stop that right now!" I shouted. "You're going to get us both in real trouble!"

"Wuditu!" she called to me gleefully. "It's fun. See?" she said, reaching for another pot. "Don't be so good for once. Come on," she coaxed, both arms stretched toward me, holding out my mother's clay frying pan. "Try this one."

I crept forward, longing for once to misbehave, to be a child like Lewteh. I took the *mgogo* from her hands, held it over my head, and threw it on the ground with all my might. *Crash!* The frying pan broke in pieces at my feet. Lewteh was right—it was fun! Excited, I threw some cups after it. "I never knew it could feel so good to be bad." I laughed.

"Ooooh, I'm going to tell on you, Wuditu," Lewteh teased in a singsong voice.

We each picked up more—pots, cups, plates—and before we knew it, every bit of pottery was lying broken at our feet. I plopped down beside her, suddenly exhausted. Looking at the mess we'd made, I realized that this was the first time in my whole life that I'd dared to be anything but responsible. I marveled at my little sister's bravery. Where did she get such courage?

We sidled into Melkeh's house as though we'd just left. Melkeh is Lewteh's mother and my stepmother. Like a lot of children in my country, I have two mothers—my birth mother, Rahel, and my stepmother, Melkeh—and one father, Berihun. I lived with my mother and my older brother, Dawid, and my father lived nearby with his second wife,

Melkeh, and their children, all of them girls. Unlike our quiet home, their house was always busy and noisy and full of activity. My mother and I spent most of our time there. Melkeh and Rahel got along so well that if you didn't see us going to sleep at night in our separate houses, you'd think we were all one family. We ate our meals together and shared most of our chores with hardly an argument.

Like the other houses in the village, our two were round and made of mud, with a thatched roof leading upward to a spiky peak. Some people decorated their inner walls with pictures cut out from magazines, but I liked what my mother and stepmother had done much better—they'd dipped their hands in paint and pressed their palms all over the walls, giving the houses a look of hands flying upward toward the sky.

As usual, Melkeh was running from one task to another and didn't seem to have noticed our absence. My mother was here too, helping Melkeh to make the Fasika feast. She gave me a sharp look but said nothing.

Even when she had a mad face, my mother was beautiful. She had light green eyes and she was very tall and graceful, taller even than my father. People tell me that she used to be the prettiest girl in the village. I hope that people will one day say that about me.

Lewteh saw my mother's suspicious look and burst into giggles. "What are you laughing about?" My stepmother smiled at her and tweaked her braids with one hand while stretching out the other to reach the frying pan before the *kitta* bread burned. As usual, no one suspected Lewteh of anything.

"I'll do that, Melkeh," I offered. I took my place at the *mgogo*, adding the newly fried piece of *kitta* onto the pile that had already been cooked. I concentrated on pouring the batter onto the sizzling pan. Relatives would soon be arriving, and much food would be needed.

"There's a good girl, Wuditu." Melkeh smiled at me and turned away to another task.

Looking at the large jug of batter still waiting to be fried into Passover bread, I sighed. I could hear the sounds of guests arriving for the feast and I wanted to greet them. But after breaking all the pots I felt that I should make up for it by staying at the fire and finishing the cooking.

"Wuditu, how you've grown," came a deep voice from right behind me. I turned around with a wide smile and, as expected, was lifted high into the air. On the way down my arms stretched out to reach around the enormous figure of my favorite cousin.

Daniel was the largest person I knew. He had a big round belly and when he laughed—and he laughed a lot—he was so heavy the ground shook! Like my father, he was a metal worker, and he always said that he was as strong as the metal he worked with and as hot as the fire.

Whenever Daniel came to visit he always brought music with him. He'd sit on a three-legged stool with his *masenqo* between his knees, scratching his bow across its single string and singing in an unexpectedly thin, high voice. We'd all join in singing and dancing until late into the night.

Daniel and I had one thing in common. We loved to climb to a high point and look out over the fields. From high up you could see rivers of golden *tef*, our local grain, growing beside patches of bright red peppers. Daniel said that such beauty always made him burst into song. But then, it seemed that almost everything made him sing, which was one of the things I loved about him.

Sometimes we'd spot a special bird that had no name. We called it the bird from Yerusalem because it always came from the west at the beginning of the year and then flew back again after the holidays. That was where our ancestors had come from. Whenever we'd see that bird, we'd sing out to it, a song that my mother had taught me—

"*Oh, you've come from Yerusalem,*
You've been to Yerusalem,
Oh! Lucky bird!
When you go back, give our love to Yerusalem!"

Washed and dressed in my beautiful new *kemis* and *netela*, I was sitting in our tiny, one-room *mesgid*, waiting for Kes Sahalu to arrive. Right before sundown, he would go from house to house and check that there wasn't a crumb of leavened food anywhere in the village.

I sat on the ground of the synagogue with the other children, Lewteh curled up in my lap. And then, here he was, dressed all in white like me, and carrying the Orit, the ancient Bible that had been in his family for generations.

"Don't move and don't speak!" I warned Lewteh, anxious not to miss a single word. I loved to listen to Kes Sahalu, with his deep, mesmerizing voice.

In a solemn tone—but one that could still be heard, even by those who'd come late and been forced to stand outside the *mesgid* walls—he began. We all waited to hear the story of how Moses had led our people out of Egypt. But this year, his words were new.

"I have a surprise for you," he said. "Last week I received a special book from Israel." He laid the Orit down and lifted a much smaller book for all of us to see. There were pictures on the cover and I wished that I were sitting closer so I could see it better. But then Kes Sahalu surprised us again by handing the book to my brother, Dawid!

Everyone in the room murmured in shock—for a young boy to be given such a privilege on the eve of the most important holiday in the year, and he not even the son of a *kes*? But Dawid deserved this honor. He longed for Yerusalem, so much so that our father had sent him to Hebrew school in a nearby village called Ambover.

"This year is truly special," Kes Sahalu smiled, "for not only did we receive this book, but we have here three of our sons who can now read the Hebrew in it. It's the same book that Jews all over the world will be reading tonight. Surely that's a sign that next year we'll be celebrating Fasika in Yerusalem!"

I listened, spellbound, as Dawid and two other boys read from the book.

After Dawid had read, Kes Sahalu stood in silence, stroking his fine white beard as though deep in thought. Then he said, "We Beta Israel, we do not belong to this land of nettles and pain."

We all grew quiet, and even the little children settled down, their parents shushing them or gently rocking the fussy babies. This was the story that he told us year after year, the story of Fasika and its special meaning for our people.

"Many generations ago, our people dwelled in a land called Yerusalem," he began. "We were a great nation."

"Wuditu, look at Dawid." Lewteh giggled, waving her hand right in front of my face.

"Be quiet!" I hissed, tightening my arms around hers. It figured that she would be the one to speak up when even the babies were silent.

Still, I threw a quick glance in Dawid's direction. Every Fasika he looked like that—transported, as though the *kes*'s words alone could carry him away to Yerusalem. He was more convinced than any of us that one day we'd all be together in the land that God had promised us. To me, Yerusalem sounded more like a dream than a real place. But I, too, felt swept up in the *kes*'s story.

"Listen well, all of you!" Kes Sahalu said, struggling to his feet and pointing a bony finger. "I want you to remember what I'm about to tell you. When the time comes for you to go to Yerusalem, you must be ready to leave this land in the blink of an eye. And when you get there, your lives will be changed forever!"

To this day, when I look back to that time I feel a terrible longing, wishing that I could change what was to come.

Chapter 2

Dibebehar, 1986

Wuditu, 10, and Lewteh, 7

Every Sunday, my brother, Dawid, set off for school with two of my cousins, and our house would feel much too empty and quiet until they came back again at the end of the week, just in time for the Sabbath.

Whenever the three set out, my mother would start to pray for their safe return. And she didn't stop praying until she saw them come home again on Friday afternoon. "What are you so worried about, Enutie?" I asked one day after watching her shake her head until I thought it would fall off.

"The road is filled with thieves," she mumbled and started praying all over again. Even though she didn't say it, I knew that she was also worried about the dangers the boys might encounter if people on the road discovered that they were Jews.

One day, my mother's fears were realized. Dawid came running home from Ambover, sweating heavily and out of breath. I drew near, wondering what he was doing coming home in the middle of the week—and why he was all by himself! Where were my two cousins?

"What's the matter? Are you sick?" my mother cried.

"A terrible thing has happened!" he said. "The government has closed all the Hebrew schools. Now it's against the law to teach Hebrew or even to speak it. The teachers have all been arrested and we've heard that they're being tortured. Some of them may already be dead!"

"Where are our sons?" my aunts demanded.

"In jail," he answered sadly. I could see that he had been crying.

"How did you get away?" my mother asked as my stepmother ran to comfort my aunts.

"I hid," he said, looking down in shame.

There was a moment of silence and then Dawid said urgently, "Father, with your permission, I must leave quickly, before they come after me too."

"Why would they come after you?" my father asked, bewildered.

"Abatie, they're arresting all the students!"

"Why would they do that?" My father shook his head in disbelief. The students were our future, he always said.

"They think that the students are all trying to overthrow our Marxist government. And they say that the Jews are even worse than the students. They say that we're traitors because we want to leave the country to go to Israel, instead of staying to fight the rebels. Father, this is a serious matter. It is treason they are talking about."

I felt the breath leave my body. Treason! Even I knew that you could be shot for that. Even little children knew that.

"Where will you go?" my mother asked.

"To Sudan," he whispered.

My mother nodded her head as though she had expected him to say this. When I saw the look in her eyes I realized that she was afraid that she might never see Dawid again.

Money and food were quickly brought for Dawid's journey. Within an hour of his return to the village, he was ready to leave.

"Will I ever see you again?" I cried, clinging to him. I couldn't seem to let go of his legs. He was already much taller than me, even though there were only four years between us.

"Of course you will, Wuditu," he answered. He was trying to be patient with me, but I could feel his fear. "I'll write to you," he promised.

I didn't have the heart to remind him that I didn't know how to read.

"Here," he said, placing a shiny silver coin on my palm. "This coin is called a Maria Theresa thaler. Keep it for the day you go to Yerusalem and use it when you need it most. *Aizosh*—be brave, Wuditu," he said, kissing me good-bye.

I looked at the coin in my palm—it was the first money I'd ever been given. None of the children in the village had ever been given any money or anything of any value at all—certainly nothing like this! It was special for another reason—this was the prize that my brother had won for being the best student in his Hebrew class. It might have helped him on his journey but he had chosen to give it to me.

I watched through my tears until he was out of my sight. After we could no longer see him, Lewteh kissed my cheek and whispered, "Wuditu, don't cry. God will watch over Dawid, you'll see."

She wanted to comfort me, but I needed to be alone with my tears and grief. I ran away and hid for most of that day, and thought about Dawid. I frowned, remembering the long-ago moment when we first realized that being a Jew set us apart in ways that could be dangerous. I think it was that day that changed everything for my brother.

This is what happened: One day, some people came to buy the things we made. Although we always nodded and bowed politely to our Christian neighbors when we passed each other and sometimes even helped each other out in times of trouble, we never shared bread or drank *buna*—our coffee—together. And when the Christianos came to buy things, they rarely brought their children with them.

But that day, a small boy had come along with two women who wanted some of my mother's pottery. Dawid had just started to play with him when the boy's mother whispered to the other woman: "Quick! Hide the child! Don't let the *falasha* eat him! You—*kayla*," the woman hissed at Dawid. "*Undat belay*, don't look at my son!"

Dawid ran away, crying and afraid, and I followed close by. We were too little to understand what was happening, so our mother explained it to us.

"They think you can make yourself into a *kayla*, a hyena, and eat a whole person—just by looking at them," Rahel said with a mocking smile, to show us how ridiculous she thought it was. "If you don't look directly at them, they won't bother you."

Chapter 3

Dibebehar, 1986

Wuditu, 10, and Lewteh, 7

Lewteh and I were up early the next morning, fetching water from the stream. As usual, she was chattering away, but, for once, I was too depressed to pay much attention to her. That night, our house had seemed so quiet without my brother, and that's how it would be from now on. At least when he was in school, I'd been able to see him on the weekends.

I started in surprise when Lewteh nudged me in the stomach and shouted, "Look, Wuditu—soldiers!"

I looked up and saw a troop of soldiers marching straight for Dibebehar. My first thought was that they might be coming because of Dawid. What if they'd caught him? Amlak Israel! Had they come to tell us that he was arrested—or dead?

We raced frantically back toward the village and on the way we met my father, who was just setting out for the fields.

"*Wotader'och*—soldiers, Father!" Lewteh and I both said, breathlessly. "They're coming right here!"

"*Kwayu*, shush, Wuditu, Lewteh! Let's see what they want before you start crying," he said and shooed us into the house where my mother and stepmother were busy clearing away the remains of my sisters' meal. From the doorway, I watched as the soldiers bypassed our neighbors' houses and marched straight toward us.

It wasn't the first time I'd seen soldiers. As long as I could remember, Ethiopia had been at war. First the rebels came and conquered our village. Then the government soldiers came and took it back. Some people in the village think that the rebels might be back again one day!

Unlike the government soldiers I'd seen at the roadblocks and in the marketplace, this group was ragged and dirty and dressed in a combination of uniform and civilian clothes. Some of them looked only a few years older than me. But they had a lot of weapons and a look in their eyes that made me uneasy, as though they wanted to frighten us. I wondered if boys so young could be trusted to carry such big, angry-looking guns.

"Those aren't soldiers," my father hissed, as he watched them approach. "They don't look like rebels either. They look like *shifta'och*—bandits. Girls, stay well out of sight!"

Bandits! The soldiers could be cruel, but the bandits—they were much worse. My sisters and I stood, terrified, peering out from inside the doorway.

My father bowed as the band of men approached.

"I'm told that you have some influence in this village," one of them said. His tone was unpleasant and he looked my father up and down in a disrespectful manner.

My father bowed again and remained silent.

"Tell your people that we are hungry," he said. "Every household in this village must provide us with food. Anyone who is not prepared to do so will be punished."

My father spoke to him in a quiet voice, bargaining over how much food each household had to give them. While they were speaking, one or two of his men left the group and spread out through the village.

Suddenly, an argument broke out in the house next to ours. One of the men had found a jug of *tela* and was waving it playfully at his comrades. He was just raising it to his lips to drink when their leader left our father's side and ran toward the man, shouting curses.

"Didn't I order you to stay together?" he yelled. "Didn't I say that everything must be done in an orderly fashion?" His rage was terrifying but after a minute or two he quieted down, looked at the thief and said in a sorrowful tone, "I told you all not to steal, didn't I?" He sighed heavily. "Now, look what I'll have to do."

At his signal, two of the men grabbed the thief and forced him to lie down on his back, stretching his arms out to the sides. I was trembling and I could feel my sisters' fear, too. Wubalu, the oldest and the most religious, was praying, and Lewteh was clinging to me. What were they going to do? Were they going to whip the man? I hoped not. He was babbling wildly and kept trying to get up but the men held him fast. The others stood around him, silent and grim.

"This is what we do to thieves," their leader shouted to all who could hear. Before I could put a hand over Lewteh's eyes, he pulled out his sword and sliced off the man's right hand at the wrist.

I stared, astonished, as the fingers continued to move, even after the hand lay separate on the ground. "Look away," I told myself, aware of a faint screaming, as though from a distance.

It's Lewteh screaming, I realized. If I didn't keep her quiet, the man might come back to our house. I picked her up off the ground, folded her into my body, and rocked her, grateful to have something to concentrate on besides that terrible moving hand.

"Hush, Lewteh," I said over and over. As her screaming became fainter, the young man's crying grew louder and louder. I remained sitting on the ground with Lewteh in my arms, trying to block out all sound, while the men took their wounded comrade out of the village and the adults gathered together, speaking softly.

Eventually someone must have put us to bed because the next thing I knew, it was morning and Melkeh was bending over the fire pit, coaxing yesterday's buried embers back to life, as though nothing unusual had happened the day before.

We'd barely finished our morning meal when another group of men came marching into the village. This time it was government soldiers and when our father motioned to us girls to go deep into the house, I grabbed Lewteh and dragged her inside, well prepared to put a hand over her eyes if the need arose. I prayed quietly to myself, "Yxaviher, let it not be about my brother. Let them not take any of our boys to the army."

I was trying to think of other things to pray for. But I stopped praying, surprised when I saw that the soldiers seemed to be in a happy mood. They spoke to the head of each household, clapping people on the back and smiling widely, before moving on to the next. I'd never seen soldiers behaving like this before!

"We heard that you had a bit of trouble here yesterday," said one of the soldiers to my father. From the shiny buttons on his coat I could tell that he was an officer.

Berihun nodded and the officer said, "I'm sorry to hear it. But don't worry. We will catch those cursed bandits and anything that they've stolen will be returned to you," he promised.

"Thank you, sir, but that's not necessary. Nothing was stolen," my father answered.

"Very well. You've probably noticed that we've been cleaning up the old school building here in the village," the officer said. "We've come to register all the adults for school. Mengistu has decided that all Ethiopia's farmers must learn to read." I knew that Mengistu was our leader.

My father bowed again and said, "Sir, officer, we are grateful to Mengistu for this wonderful opportunity. But we have too much work to do in the fields."

"So, *falasha* devil, you would like to disobey Mengistu's orders?" the officer asked grimly, his good humor vanishing in an instant.

"No, sir, of course not, I will do as Mengistu wishes." My father bowed again. I was relieved to see the officer's smile return to his face.

"Tomorrow you will all report to the school, yes?" the

officer said and stayed silent until my father had nodded his agreement.

The next morning Melkeh watched my father getting ready to start out for the fields, as though the officer had never issued his orders.

"What shall we do about the school?" she asked anxiously.

"With all that needs to be done, I don't have time to study. I won't be going to school," my father said firmly.

"What if they come back and find that we haven't obeyed?" my mother whispered fearfully.

"Melkeh, Rahel, girls—you know, I would have liked us all to go," my father answered earnestly. "I sent my only son to school because I believed that it was important for him to learn. Didn't our neighbors laugh at me for sending away such a strapping boy who could have helped me in the fields? But now that he's gone, how can I go to school? Who will harvest the crops? Who will make the tools? How will we eat if no one does the work?"

He thought for a moment and then said to my stepmother, "Melkeh, you will represent us at the school." To my mother, he said, "Rahel, you and I and the girls—we will all carry on with our work."

I listened quietly to my father's words, but I was aching to speak up for myself. Ever since Dawid had first gone to school I'd wanted so badly to go too. But there was no point in my even asking—my father would never have allowed one of his daughters to walk all that way with a war going on. But now there would be a school right here in our village! A chance like this might never come again!

"Oh, Abatie, I want to go too—may I please?" I begged.

"It's a school for adults," my father pointed out. "Are you an adult?"

"No," I answered, thinking furiously. I threw a glance at my mother, hoping that she would say something in my favor. But then I thought of a way to persuade him. "I'm tall for my age," I reasoned. "If you agree to send me, there will be two of us and the soldiers will see that we've tried our best to obey their orders."

My father looked at my older sisters, Wubalu and Aster, and my heart fell. I waited while he shifted from one foot to the other, thinking.

"I need the older girls to help me in my work," he decided. "*Ishi*, all right—Wuditu, you may go with your stepmother."

Mulu'alem, the youngest of my sisters, started to say something but kept silent when she saw my stepmother shaking her head.

"I'm tall. I want to go to school too," Lewteh whined and then stamped her foot when everyone laughed. No one bothered to point out that she was half my size!

"You will stay and help your mother and your sisters," my father told Lewteh, and despite the horrible faces she made behind our father's back, I knew that Lewteh would do as he wished.

It was only a few minutes' walk to where the old one-room school stood. But it seemed to take forever. Ever since I'd woken up that morning, I'd been waiting impatiently for just this moment.

"Wuditu, stop it!" my stepmother scolded when for the third or fourth time in as many minutes my whirling and skipping nearly pushed her into a ditch.

"I'm sorry, I'm just so excited! I'm going to school!" I smiled hugely at her.

"Humph," she muttered. "You'd better tell your long legs to settle down before they get you into trouble. How are you going to learn anything if you keep bouncing around like that? Hurry up, they're ringing the bell!"

When we entered the building, we saw that there were more people than chairs so many of the adults were standing in rows at the back of the room. I'd imagined that the teacher would be old and maybe have a long beard, like our *kes*. But he was a young man. He was thin and he kept shivering and hunching down into his jacket, although it wasn't cold. Despite his young age, he had an extremely high forehead. But his smile was so wide and bright that you didn't really notice his bald head.

"Welcome, everyone," he said, warmly. "I'm your teacher, Yosef. I know it's been a difficult season for you farmers and I'm happy that you've made time for this important matter. As you know, Mengistu, our great Marxist leader, has decided that all the farmers in Ethiopia must learn to read. That's why we're holding these classes in the late afternoon, so that you'll have time to tend to your fields. I'm confident that we will all make great progress. Let us begin."

I liked the teacher immediately, but as I listened to his speech, I wondered whether he knew that we'd been ordered to come to his class. I also worried about what he might do when he realized I was the only child in the room. My height must have fooled him because he didn't say anything. He just nodded when I said my name.

I need not have worried. From the very first lesson Yosef paid me special attention and praised me often. Since most of the adults in our village had never held a pen or pencil in their hands, the teacher gave us a choice—we could either make the letters out of clay or we could embroider them on small pieces of cloth. I thought this was very clever of him. My stepmother and I chose to work with clay since we already knew how to handle it. We only needed to learn how to shape the letters.

After a few weeks, most of the adults were still repeating the letters that Yosef wrote on the board. He'd point to the letters, say them out loud, and the students would repeat after him—over and over again, all through the lesson. It was hard for the adults. They were tired after their long day in the fields, and every once in a while, one of them would start to snore!

Yosef was a very patient teacher. He never reprimanded the students for falling asleep in class. Even though most of them weren't learning very much, we were patient with him too because we all thought he was such a good person.

Unlike the others, I was already starting to sound out whole words. But I had a head start. After he'd begun to study in Ambover, Dawid had taught me all the letters. Even after he left the village, I'd continued to practice them over and over, using a stick in the dirt.

"That's very good, Wuditu!" Yosef said approvingly. "If you keep on like this, I'll lend you one of my books to take home."

My stepmother hugged me proudly and the other adults smiled their approval. I imagined myself walking through the village with a book tucked under my arm. What respect everyone would have for me! The only other person who did this was the *kes*. He was very learned and carried his Orit, his Bible, everywhere he went.

As time went on, I noticed that my stepmother was still struggling. She had no trouble forming the letters in clay, but when Yosef called her to the blackboard she didn't seem to understand that the clay forms on the desk and the letters written in chalk were the same. Many of the other adults were having the same problem, and I wished that I could help. I usually sat in a corner reading books that Yosef brought me while he struggled to teach the adults.

I felt sorry for him. He'd started out with such great hopes for us. One day I saw a broken piece of chalk on the floor and it gave me an idea. I quickly took it and pushed it into a fold in my *netela*. I knotted the cloth around it to hold it in place. I wasn't sure whether it was wrong to do it, but I really wanted to help Melkeh learn to read.

That afternoon, I found her by the stream and wrote a few letters on some large, flat stones. I'd already tried to draw some letters in the sand for her with a stick, but she still didn't get it. Now I was excited because I thought that the white chalk marks on black stones would be much more like the chalk marks on the blackboard. And here we could take our time. We didn't have to hurry to please the teacher.

I was right! She recognized the letters right away!

"I get so upset when everyone is looking at me, Wuditu," she confessed. "I can barely see the letters. But please don't take any more chalk. You know it is wrong, don't you?"

"I know, Melkeh. But it fell to the floor. And the teacher's hands are too big to hold it—look how small it is."

"Maybe you should be our teacher, Wuditu." Melkeh laughed. "You're the only child in the school and look how well you are doing."

One day, the teacher took me aside and said, "Wuditu, I've been watching you. You've already learned everything I'll be teaching this year and now there's nothing for you to do but read books. There's only one of me here and so many students. I was wondering if you'd like to be my helper."

"Oh, yes, sir!" I said eagerly. I'd been longing to help. It seemed silly for me to be sitting around reading when the others were having such a difficult time. Over the next few weeks, Yosef would choose a different student for me to help each day. I'd take that person aside, drag two chairs to the back of the classroom, and start to work with them.

At first I was hesitant about teaching the adults. I worried that they might feel embarrassed to be taught by a young girl. But I saw that it was just the opposite. They were humiliated that they'd made so little progress and were happy to have my help. When they, too, began to read I was so proud!

At home, I was continuing to teach my stepmother and both my mother and Lewteh had joined our lessons. They were learning as quickly as I had. My father encouraged me to read a story to everyone on Saturdays, but he felt that teaching was work, so I only did that during the week.

Finally, one day it happened. The teacher caught me stealing a bit of chalk and scolded me in front of the whole class.

"What were you planning to do with this?" he asked

sternly, holding up the evidence of my crime for all to see.

"Sir, I wanted to teach the children in the village what you are teaching us," I replied tearfully.

"And what would you be writing on?" he asked, knowing very well that we were too poor to own any paper. "Were you going to sell the chalk?"

"No, sir, I wouldn't do that. I was going to write on stones," I answered in a barely audible voice. My stepmother stared apprehensively at Yosef, and the whole class waited to see what he would say.

"Very well, you may keep the chalk," he said and made me promise never to steal anything again. I worried that I would have to bear the worst punishment of all—having shamed my parents. But they said nothing about the incident and smiled proudly whenever they saw me teaching my sisters to draw their names in the dirt.

Chapter 4

Dibebehar, 2 years later, 1988

Wuditu, 12, and Lewteh, 9

I was now considered the best reader in the village, and people had started asking me to read their letters to them. The arrival of a letter was a very important event, and sometimes I was asked to read them out loud to the whole village. But there were other letters that were passed to me secretly, and I knew that they must be read in whispers, inside people's homes. They were from Israel, and when they first began to arrive and there was nothing from Dawid, we all feared that only something terrible would have prevented him from writing to us.

"The walk to Sudan was long and difficult," one such letter revealed. "Bandits stopped us on the way, robbed us, and left us with no food or water. The whole time, we had to hide from the government soldiers because we didn't have a travel pass. Once or twice they nearly caught us. If they had, God knows what they would have done to us! Then, when we got to Sudan, we found that people were dying from the terrible diseases in the refugee camps and we had to wait many months before our turn came to go to Yerusalem."

But the letters also described Yerusalem as a land of beauty and freedom and said that we must all make a great effort to get there. One day a letter arrived with news so astonishing that for weeks I lay awake at night, wondering if it could really be true.

It said: "A messenger will come soon to guide you to freedom." When I read that, it renewed my hopes for Dawid and for all of us.

Our teacher was so pleased with the progress of the adult class that he asked the *kabele*, the local administration, for permission to teach the children from all the local villages. I was delighted to hear this, thinking that now I would have a chance to study with kids my own age. But, as usual, the representative from the *kabele* had his own ideas.

"Where does the learned teacher expect to put the children?" he asked sarcastically, looking at the crowded classroom.

But Yosef was a patient and determined man, and in time he persuaded the *kabele* that the classes could be divided: the children could study in the morning and the adults in the afternoon.

Kids came to the school from all the nearby villages, and I soon realized that I was the only one in the class who was Beta Israel. Many of our older youths had run away to

Sudan, and the younger ones were desperately needed in the fields. But whenever anyone protested that I, too, could be helping at home, my father always insisted that I must continue to study.

One morning the teacher came into the classroom and hung a row of large photographs on the board. He talked about the different tribes in Ethiopia, then pointed to one of the photographs and said, "That is a *falasha* woman. The *falashas* are different from the other tribes. Does anyone know what makes the *falashas* different from all the other people in Ethiopia?"

I was about to put up my hand and answer that we alone had come from the Promised Land, but I saw in the teacher's face that he had something very exciting to say and I held back, thinking, He wants to tell us himself.

"The *falashas* are the only ones who are *buda*—possessors of the evil eye," he said. I was shocked. It was a good thing I hadn't put up my hand!

"You may have been in their villages and perhaps your parents have bought their pottery or their woven goods. Or maybe your father needed some tools and he went to the *falashas* for that," he continued.

Several children nodded their heads.

"Do any of your mothers know how to make pots?" he asked. No one answered.

"Do any of your fathers know how to work with metal?" Again, no one answered. The girl in the seat next to me turned her head to look at me and I thought, Does she know that I am Beta Israel?

"Of course not!" the teacher said, nearly bouncing up

and down in his eagerness to explain. "There's only one way a person can learn things like that. And do you know how?" he asked. Still, no one answered.

"Through an evil spirit!" he hissed dramatically, and the children shrank backward in their seats. "Only through an evil spirit can that knowledge be passed on from generation to generation. I caution you to keep your distance from the people who work with fire," he warned. "They have evil in them and can harm you just by looking at you!"

I squirmed in my seat, not knowing what to do. I thought that everyone must be looking at me. But no, they were all looking at the teacher, except for Hailu, the girl next to me. While Yosef was speaking, she kept edging her chair farther away from me and closer to the boy in the next row.

Was I really hearing this—in school? Did even my beloved teacher believe these terrible stories about us? And now he was teaching others to think the same way. How could a learned person do that?

"Isn't it true that the *falashas* killed our Lord?" Hailu asked, with a sly glance at me.

"Yes, that's true," Yosef answered. "It was many years ago, but we do have proof of this. And do you know what that is?"

No one answered. I sat still, barely breathing. What new evil did these people think we had committed? Was there no end to their insanity?

"How did our Lord die?" the teacher asked.

"He died on the cross," one of the students answered promptly.

"And how did his body stay on the cross?" Yosef asked.

"Why didn't it fall off?"

"He was nailed to it," one of the students answered.

"Aha! And who is it who makes the nails?" Yosef asked, pleased.

I didn't have to wait for the answer. He was right. It was my people who made the nails. Murder of their Lord! That was a very serious charge. My stomach lurched and I prayed that I wouldn't be sick.

When I got home from school that day, I told my mother what had happened. The thought of being in a classroom where others—even my teacher—could think such things of me filled me with dread. And yet I had loved going to school until this very day, and the thought of not returning because of other people's ignorance made me angry!

"It is so unfair," I said tearfully to my mother.

"But, Wuditu, what if this continues?" my mother said. I could hear the fear in her voice. I knew that it was the same fear she'd had for Dawid when he went away to Ambover. "What if something worse happens?"

I knew that my mother was right, and that I shouldn't go back. But that night, I lay awake for a long time, one minute angry, the next afraid. What should I do?

That night, my mother came to my bedside. She lay beside me and very quietly asked, "Do you remember why I gave you the name Wuditu?"

I pretended to be asleep. Was my mother really going to tell me this old story again?

She waited, and it was clear that she expected an answer.

I sighed and opened my eyes. "Because Wuditu means

'little treasure' and I am your treasure."

"That's right, child. And do you know what else I have given you?" she asked.

"My neck," I said.

"Yes, that's right," she said, squeezing my hand. "Your grandmother Tarik was tall like me and she had a wonderful long neck. The children used to tease her, calling her the girl with the neck of a giraffe."

I had always loved this part of the story, and I couldn't help but smile.

"Tarik has been gone a long time," she said wistfully. "But sometimes, even now, when people see you walking around the village, they still say, 'Look—there goes Tarik's long-necked granddaughter!'"

She was quiet for a minute. When she spoke again, her voice was not wistful. It was steady and unwavering. "Sometimes, there is so much sorrow in this life that we forget how strong we are. We know how to bear our sorrows, Wuditu. When bad times come, we pray that if we are patient, things will get better. Isn't that right?"

I nodded, wondering if she was speaking more to me or to herself.

"You are a brave girl, Wuditu. You are like your brother. Whatever happens, whatever you decide about school, remember the giraffe—she has a long neck and she's beautiful. Even when she's sad or frightened, she holds her head up and she doesn't cry—not even when life seems too hard to bear."

In the morning, I returned to school. It was an ordinary day, and it felt as though everything that had happened the day before was a bad dream. Still, I knew that it wasn't a dream, and I could not feel as I had before. As though to remind me, Hailu made a point of turning her back on me whenever I came near her. And whenever she did, I remembered to hold my head high.

Chapter 5

Dibebehar, 1988

Wuditu, 12, and Lewteh, 9

It wasn't only at school where I felt uneasy about being a Jew. Even though I was only a child, I understood that the government was also making life very difficult for the Beta Israel. It seemed like every few weeks there was a new law or change that had to do with us.

Recently, we'd started out for market with our baskets—just like any other market day. When we got to town we were surprised to find that there was no one there.

"What happened to the market?" my father asked a passing stranger.

"Major Melaku changed the market day to Saturday," the man replied, referring to the governor of Gondar Province.

We all stood, shocked, unable to take this in. This was a terrible blow. Our laws forbade us to work or even to travel on Sabbath. How would we bring our goods to the market?

"Do you know why Major Melaku changed the market day?" my father asked.

"Major Melaku knows that the *falashas* sell their goods on market day. He hates your people and knows that this will make it harder for you." The man lowered his voice. "Some of us think it wasn't fair to do this. But what can we do? Nothing! We have no power."

"Now we'll have to pay someone to sell our goods," my father answered grimly. "There will be less profit for us."

"These are not good times for your people." The stranger bowed politely and walked off, shaking his head.

Our walk back to Dibebehar was a sad one. The road was steep and we climbed it with heavy feet. I couldn't help comparing this journey with the last time we'd been to market. My father had bought a special fruit for my sisters and me. We'd carefully peeled it and separated it into pieces, two for each of us. I'd never tasted such a fruit before. It was sweet and tart at the same time. I kept the taste on my tongue and savored it, refusing to drink water along the way so that it would stay in my mouth as long as possible.

"What was that fruit we had last time, Abatie?" I asked as we walked dejectedly back to our village. I hoped to cheer him up.

"*Birtukan*, it was an orange," he answered.

"The fruit has the same name as the color," I said.

"That's right, Wuditu, just like the color," my father replied. But I could tell that his mind was on this new problem that we now faced.

After a few quiet months at school, things began to get worse. Each day came with some new unpleasantness, and it was always Hailu who started the trouble. Sometimes she just called me names, like *buda* or *kayla* or anything else that she could think of.

One day Hailu smirked at me the entire morning, and when I started to walk home I found a group of girls waiting for me.

"Here she is," Hailu shouted, and before I could defend myself, the girls had pulled me to the ground and were kicking and punching me. "You killed our Lord," they yelled. "You must be punished for that!"

I don't know where my strength came from or the terrible anger that took me over. "I never killed anyone in my life and I never will!" I yelled. I grabbed one of Hailu's legs and pulled her to the ground. I punched her and pulled her braids until I thought they would come out of her head.

While Hailu was crying and the rest of the girls were all standing still, shocked by the suddenness of my attack, I scrambled up and ran all the way home.

"What happened to you, Wuditu?" my mother asked when I ran, breathing heavily, into the house. Tearfully, I related what had happened. "Perhaps it would be better if you didn't go anymore," my mother suggested.

"No, I want to stay in school," I answered stubbornly. "Why should I let that girl put an end to my education?"

That night, I lay sleepless in my bed. I remembered my fight with Hailu and couldn't believe that was me, fighting back. I was a little afraid of what might happen the next day at school. But I also knew that I was going to go to school and nothing, not Hailu and her friends or Yosef and his ignorant lessons on Beta Israel, would stop me.

I was on my way home from school a few days later when Lewteh came running to meet me.

"What's happened?" I asked, worried to see her so out of breath.

"I don't know. But Father says there is a surprise at home and he sent me to meet you. We must hurry!" Lewteh grabbed my hand and we ran home.

As soon as I came into the house, I could see that everyone was gathered together in a huddle around someone. My mother stood beside him, holding his hand. Looking more closely, I realized the man was Dawid!

I threw myself into my brother's arms and we held each other for a long time. Stepping back to look at him, I realized that in the time he'd been away he'd grown tall, like our mother. What a beautiful man he'd become! I looked at him admiringly, but I was also afraid. Where had he been all this time? Why had he come back? Wasn't it dangerous for him to be here? I had so many questions stored up for so long.

With Lewteh sitting in my lap and my sisters on the ground all around me, we listened raptly to Dawid as he spoke about his life since he had left Dibebehar. He'd walked for weeks before reaching Sudan. After he arrived, he'd waited a long time in a refugee camp, and then one night he was taken secretly into the desert by men from

Yerusalem. Planes had come out of the sky and landed in the middle of nowhere! He spoke with a confidence I'd never heard before.

"Before I knew it, soldiers wearing foreign uniforms came running out and herded us into the planes. People whispered to one another, 'They are soldiers from Yerusalem!'

"We flew for hours and I was very sick. I threw up all over one of the soldiers." He laughed. "Then we landed in Israel." We all gasped.

"Is that where you've been all this time?" my father asked.

Dawid nodded. "Yes. I studied for a few months and then a man asked me if I would like to help my people get to Israel. How could I refuse?" he added with a smile.

"Father, I must ask your forgiveness," Dawid said. "I didn't just arrive. I've been in Ethiopia for a while. I've been to many villages, giving people instructions. But until now I wasn't allowed to come to my own village. These were my orders," he said with a guilty shrug.

"Finally, I told my superiors that I could no longer bear it. How could I stay in Ethiopia and not try to help my own family? Please, Father, say that you forgive me for not having come sooner. I have felt great pain over this!"

"You were working for a holy cause, son," my father said, which seemed to be enough to ease Dawid's burden.

My brother took a long breath and looked intently at all of us. "The time is now," he said.

Chapter 6

Dibebehar, 1988

Wuditu, 12, and Lewteh, 9

My gasp was echoed by others all around the room. The time had come for us to follow my brother to Israel! I was so excited that my whole body shivered and I had to make a great effort to listen to my brother's instructions. He explained that there was famine in parts of the country. Thousands of people were fleeing to Sudan, where they were being fed in refugee camps.

"The State of Israel is asking you to make the trek to Sudan," my brother explained. "They know that it is a long and dangerous trip. But it is the only way for you to get to the Holy Land. Make your arrangements to leave as soon as possible. But go quietly," he instructed. "Don't let anyone suspect that you are planning to leave Ethiopia.

"Here's money for the journey," he said, handing my father a thick envelope. "Perhaps you might use some of it to buy yourselves new clothes. That way, it will appear as though you are going to a wedding or a feast and the soldiers won't suspect that you're trying to leave the country."

My father nodded soberly.

"When you get to Sudan," Dawid instructed, "hide yourselves among the other refugees. You may have to wait a long time for your turn to leave, and the wait will not be easy nor the conditions good."

"My brother Alemu left a few months ago with his family. Do you know if he was taken to Yerusalem?" my father asked.

"I don't think so," Dawid replied. "But I've been here for a while. If he is still in Sudan, he'll be able to help you. May God protect you on your journey," he said, and a few minutes later he was gone.

This time there was none of the pain I'd felt when he'd run away after the Hebrew schools had closed. I would be seeing him very soon in Yerusalem.

We planned to leave in one month. Over the next few weeks, my father sold all our animals—but one at a time, so no one would guess that we were leaving. Father said that Melkeh and I must continue to go to school and do our chores as though nothing unusual was going to happen. We were not to talk, even among ourselves, about our plans. "Not a word," my father said sternly. "With our neighbors constantly coming into the village to buy one thing or another, you never know when the wrong people might be listening."

In the evenings, my mother and I sewed birr notes into the seams of our clothes. My stepmother did the same. We'd received a lot of money from Dawid so there was a lot to hide. As we worked, we stayed well back from the doorway, even though the light from the fire was much stronger there. My mother smiled more than usual and hugged me often, and there were nights when it took us a long time to fall asleep. Because of this I was often tired during the day, and my mind would wander.

On what was to be my last day at school, Yosef took me aside and looked at me with a puzzled expression. "What is the matter with you lately, Wuditu?" he asked coolly. "You have not been paying attention. I wonder what could be on your mind that is so much more important than your studies."

"There's nothing on my mind, sir," I answered.

"Do you no longer care about learning?"

"Of course I do, sir," I answered. My heart was beating wildly. Was my behavior making him suspicious?

"Then tell me, please, what has caused you to be so inattentive," Yosef persisted. "Might you be bored with your lessons?"

"Oh no, I'm not, sir!" I answered.

"Might you be going on a trip, perhaps?" he asked.

"Going on a trip? Of course not, sir," I answered, praying that he didn't see how terrified I was becoming. I tried to think of a reason to give him for my sudden lack of interest. But I couldn't come up with anything. Finally, I did think of something. "I'm going to be married soon," I blurted out and lowered my eyes to the ground.

All the way home I worried. Why had he asked me if I was going on a trip? Did he suspect? What if he didn't believe me? What if he asked my parents about my getting married and discovered that I was lying? If he did, I knew that he could be dangerous. He could report us to the *kabele*!

When I arrived home I found that the village was full of people, and many were asking why there were so few things to buy. As though they suspected that we were leaving, they crowded into our area, anxious to buy whatever we had left. I stayed close to home for most of that afternoon, afraid that I might say or do something that would increase suspicions against us. Before I went to sleep, I thanked God that Yosef hadn't come and I prayed that nothing would stop us from leaving the next day!

On the morning of our departure, my father woke us early, before the sun had even come up. We dressed in the new clothes that he had bought for us in the market. My sisters and I looked each other over excitedly. Our dresses were pure white and the edges were trimmed with colored threads—mine even had golden ones! The patterns were much more complicated than the ones our weavers made.

But the cloth was much stiffer than ours and would be much less comfortable against our skin. I didn't know how we were supposed to keep our dresses clean on the long trip through the mountains. But the important thing was that no one would expect a group of people so well dressed to be setting out on a long journey, as my father reminded us. "If anyone should stop you or question you, tell them we're going to a family wedding."

I was too excited to be hungry, but my father saw me sitting with my hands by my side and urged, "Eat, Wuditu—eat until you're full. It's going to be a long day and we may not be able to eat before nightfall."

All at once I realized that this was our last meal in Dibebehar! I got up to help clear everything away. But

Berihun said to leave it all where it was. I looked at my father in surprise.

"Leave it all?" I asked, looking at the dirty plates, stained bright red with spicy lentil stew. I looked at my stepmother's best coffee cups, still coated with grains of thick, black *buna*. Were we really going to leave it all like that and just walk out the door?

"That's right. Let it all just lie there," my father said with a smile. As he waved us out of the house, he touched each of us lightly on the head and murmured a quick blessing.

Part Two

Refugees

CHAPTER 7

En route to Sudan

Perhaps I should have been afraid, but I wasn't. I knew that we might face dangers on the journey—Dawid had explained that to us very clearly. But I felt safe in my father's care. He wasn't a large man—already at 12, I was almost as tall as him! But he was a man of great authority, respected even by the Christianos, who often asked him to judge their disputes. He would always protect us, no matter what lay ahead. Before we left, I gave him my precious Maria Theresa coin, the one that Dawid had given me. "Take this, Father," I said proudly. "Dawid meant for it to help us get to Yerusalem."

After a whole day's walking, I was already tired and hurting all over. I was longing for a rest, but I didn't want to be the first one to complain. I wanted to show everyone how strong I was, how willing to help. Wubalu and Aster were big and didn't seem to be tiring. And Mulu'alem, the youngest, was being carried most of the way by my stepmother. I kept an eye on Lewteh, who was struggling to keep up on the steep and treacherous mountain paths and wearing shoes for the first time. I could tell from the way she walked that her feet hurt. But like the brave girl she was, she didn't complain and I praised her often.

We were heading first for Cousin Daniel's village. I was so happy that he and his family would be coming with us—along with the guide that he'd hired to show us the way. The next evening we would set out to the west—toward Sudan. From then on, we'd walk at night and hide during the day from soldiers and bandits.

As we walked, my mother sang her song about the bird from Yerusalem and we all chimed in. "Wuditu, I've thought about this day so often," she confessed, "but I never really believed that it would come to pass. When I was a little girl, we used to speak of going to Yerusalem. My parents had spoken of going but they never left Ethiopia. Every year at Fasika, my grandparents had said, 'Next year in Yerusalem,' but they had died without going there. Their parents before them had died and never gone. And so, it seemed to me that all my life I would pray to go to Yerusalem, but I would most probably die without ever getting there."

We searched the skies but saw no sign of the bird from Yerusalem. It was a bit early in the season for him to appear.

I'd just turned around to check on Lewteh when she stopped abruptly, nearly toppling her mother, who was coming up behind her. "What's that noise?" Lewteh asked, looking uneasily up at the sky.

"I don't hear anything," I answered, but barely a moment passed before a swarm of planes came into view, flying low.

"Quick! Hide!" my father shouted, and as one, we threw ourselves down the side of a ravine. As I dove under cover of the bushes, brambles tore at my skin. The planes swooped around us and I held my breath and crawled even deeper into the undergrowth, trying to protect my face and eyes while what seemed like hundreds of sharp needles dug into my body.

I could hear the planes circling and circling, as though they were looking for something. Do they think we are rebels? I wondered, hoping they'd see our white clothes and just fly off to wherever they came from. But then bombs started to fall! One exploded right near me, sending a shower of dirt onto my back! I smelled smoke and heard the crackle of fire, but with the planes still circling around us I was too frightened to move. The smell of burning seemed to be coming from close behind me! But all I could do was stay where I was and pray, "Yxaviher, save me!"

My legs ached from crouching low, and the smell of smoke grew stronger. But I held myself still and continued to pray until, after a long while, the planes flew away to the south.

There was silence and then I heard my mother and stepmother calling out, "*Lijoch*, children! Where are you?" They ran from one to the other of us, patting everyone down to be sure that we were not seriously hurt.

"Enutie, there's something on my back—what is it?" I cried, coming out from under the bushes and trying to feel behind me.

"It's nothing, child, just clumps of dirt," she said, but as she brushed off my clothes I saw that she winced, shook her fingers, and screamed, "Aiee! It's hot!"

"What is it?" I shrieked and waited while she searched under my *netela* and *kemis*. "*Ishi*, don't worry, there's nothing there," she said. "But I'm afraid your new *netela* is ruined."

"Here—take mine, I'll wear my old one," Lewteh said and I let her drape her new shawl around my shoulders.

I was shaking. I looked at the wrap my father had given me. There were black holes burned all the way through and blood stained the beautiful white material.

"Wuditu, see—you're not hurt, only scratched," my mother soothed, patting my back once again to be sure that I wasn't burned. Her hand was warm on my skin and I leaned into her neck, taking comfort from her nearness.

"*Kwayu*—be still, all of you," my father urged, mopping at a trail of blood that trickled from his head into his eyes.

"Abatie, you're hurt!" I cried out, running to his side.

"I'm okay, it's only a scratch," he said, squeezing my shoulder. "We're all fine—God has saved us! Let's get away from here before the planes return."

We climbed back up to the path, making our way carefully around the deep holes made by the bombs. I looked back to where I had been hiding. The whole area was thick with smoke and we were all coughing badly. When we stopped at the top of a hill to drink and catch our breath, I looked out over the area, wondering at how we all could have come through so much destruction without being hurt. It really was a miracle!

We climbed steadily for quite some time, and at one point I turned to look behind me and said, "I didn't thank you for the *netela*, Lewteh."

"That's all right, Wuditu, you look so pretty in it. I don't mind using my old one."

"You were very brave, Lewteh," I said.

"I know," she answered importantly, and I laughed.

Chapter 8

Chowber Village, that same evening

At the entrance to Daniel's village, we passed an abandoned hut, and through an open window I saw a blackboard. "Look, that must have been a school once," I said to Lewteh. There was a gaping tear in the roof and bullet holes on one whole side of the building. Thinking about it made me very angry! Every time soldiers came through a village, the children had to stop learning.

I was tired and hungry. And I was beginning to worry about the long walk ahead of us. Being attacked so soon after we started out seemed like a very bad sign. But at least we hadn't seen any more planes.

Daniel's family washed our hands and feet and immediately sat us down to eat and drink. "You've had a difficult journey," they said. "Now rest well. We'll be leaving tomorrow night."

"Look at what my new shoes have done!" Lewteh complained and poked at the blisters on her heels and toes.

She sighed with pleasure when her feet were washed with cool water.

"Is everything ready? Is the guide here? Is he trustworthy?" my father asked.

"He's been waiting for two days and we've heard very good things about him," Daniel assured him. "Everything is ready."

The next day we set out right after the sun set. There were 15 of us in all, including the guide and Daniel's family—his wife and their children, his wife's elderly mother and her sister. Daniel's older sons had already left for Sudan and he was hoping that we would find them there.

Because of the two old women, we moved very slowly in the dark, and whenever we'd come to a place that was steep, Daniel would carry his wife's mother and her sister, one at a time, while we waited for them to catch up. I wished he'd taken his *masenqo* as it would have cheered us up. But I knew that it would have been a hindrance on the journey.

It was the beginning of the dry season, and cracks had burst open along the path. They weren't very deep, but on that first night the moon was only a small sliver and I felt my way carefully. I knew that if I caught a foot in one of those cracks and fell, I might break a leg. How would I get to Sudan if that happened?

The route the guide took was a difficult one. I don't know what was harder—climbing up the mountains or climbing down. Both made my legs ache. I struggled to keep going, day after day. At first, I made myself think about the new life I would have in Yerusalem. But after a while, all I could think about was when we would eat and drink and when we would stop to rest. I no longer remembered thinking that the journey was going to be a great adventure.

After a few days, we finally came out of the mountains. That's better, I thought. It will be much easier to walk if we don't have to climb up or down. But I soon changed my mind when I saw that the land before us was so densely wooded that our guide had to cut a path for us through the trees. I thrashed my way through the thick undergrowth, trying to protect my eyes from low branches. I would stop, terrified, whenever I heard a rustling sound.

"What was that? What kind of animal is making that noise?" I'd gasp each time, wondering, Could it be a lion—or worse, a snake?

"Never mind, Wuditu, just keep going," my father would answer wearily.

A few days later, we came out of the forest and there before us was a vast desert—completely flat and empty. I'd never seen anything like it! Just dirt and more dirt, low bushes, and the occasional tree that was too bare either to hide us from bandits or to shelter us from the sun.

Until then, we'd had no trouble finding water. But now the guide sometimes searched for a long time before finding any, and on those days my throat closed up and my tongue stuck to my mouth. The little ones cried pitifully and Daniel sang silly songs, trying to make them laugh. My father advised, "Save your throat, there's almost no water left."

Later that night, I woke up when I heard Daniel's wife crying out, "Aiee! Daniel! Wake up! Wake up! Berihun, something's wrong. Come quick!"

He was dead. We could all see that. He lay on his back, his big belly still and his face twisted up as though in terrible pain. Even so, my father bent over him, hoping that he was still breathing "No!" he said. "God help him. He's gone."

"He's dead, just like that? Something must have killed him! He wouldn't have just died, a great big healthy man like that!" the guide said, then bent down and began searching his body. Just above his shoe, he found a bite that was red and swollen.

"Could it have been a snake? Some kind of biting insect?" my father asked, pulling at his hair in sorrow. "Why didn't he cry out for help?" he sobbed. Already, Daniel's wife was wailing and tearing her hair, and soon we were all sobbing loudly.

We all stood by while my father dug a hole in the sand, using his hands and a thick walking stick that had been with him since the beginning of our journey. When my mother and stepmother tried to help, my father pushed them out of the way.

I looked at the wilderness around me. I felt frightened and weak. If the desert could claim such a big person as Daniel, what could it do to my sisters and me? My mind raced. What would we do without Daniel? How would we get the two old women all the rest of the way to Sudan? And who would sing to us? Daniel had taken his music with him.

There was no *kes* to say prayers over the dead, but my father said a blessing and placed rocks on Daniel's grave, to prevent scavengers from finding his body. "*Kuchevalu*, sit down, all of you," he said as the guide stood anxiously by his side.

"We cannot go forward," my father told him. "We must stay here."

"For how long?" the guide asked.

"For the full seven days of mourning," my father answered.

"That's not possible! I'm sorry, but I cannot wait here for seven days. Besides, we're almost at the border," the guide urged. "Surely you can see that we have to keep going."

"It is our way," my father answered, and as we all sat down, every one of us was aware that his decision put us in grave danger. We had very little food left, but, more important, we had very little water, certainly not enough for seven days.

The guide was reluctant to argue with my father. But I knew that he wouldn't wait for us to finish the mourning period. Already he and my father had argued about traveling on the Sabbath, and my father had reluctantly agreed to go forward on those days. But getting up before the end of the mourning period would be a terrible act of disrespect. I could hardly bear to look at Daniel's wife and children. I could only be grateful that, for now, their loud wailing had stopped.

The guide waited respectfully a short distance away from us while all through the day we prayed and spoke of Daniel, of his great joy and enormous strength. The next morning, my father got up and faced the grave with his head bowed. He muttered a prayer and then said, "We must go on." His voice broke as he continued: "To get up so soon is a terrible sin and I take it all upon myself. I vow in front of all of you that when we reach Yerusalem I will make a gift to the poor in Daniel's name. I will do so every year on the day of his passing. This I swear to all of you. Now, let us go on and may God forgive us and watch over all of us."

The guide was right about our being close to the border. A few days later, we saw a flash of water shining in the distance. He stopped us and pointed. "That's the border," he said to my father. "At this time of the year, the river isn't deep and you can easily cross it. When you do, you'll be in Sudan. Soldiers will come and ask you questions. If you give them the right answers, they'll take you to a refugee camp. Tell them that your village has been bombed, that there's famine, and that your family is hungry."

The guide looked us over and warned, "You'd better not go into Sudan looking like that. Tell your people to take off their shoes and hide them. Put on your oldest, dirtiest clothes. It's very important to look poor and hungry when you are in Sudan. Don't let your women go anywhere alone. And don't ever let anyone know that you are Jews.

"I leave you here—Yxaviher be with you." The guide bowed, turned, and walked back into the vast wilderness.

We decided to spend the night by the river and cross over in the morning. After days of searching desperately for water, it was wonderful to be able to wash and drink our fill of the cool, running water. Refreshed, I changed into my oldest clothes and wrapped the rest of my things in an old *netela*. Just to be sure, I rubbed dirt over the parcel, to make it look even more worn.

The next morning, my father gathered us together and, without a backward glance for the land of our birth, led us safely across the river into Sudan and toward the soldiers waiting to receive us.

Chapter 9

Sudan–Ethiopia border, the next morning

"Wait here," my father ordered.

I stood still and watched as he approached the border post. He bowed deeply to the soldiers, his nose nearly touching the ground. He looked everywhere but at the soldiers. I was surprised and a little ashamed to see him behaving so humbly, like a man with no status and no hope. Why was my proud father behaving this way?

I felt uneasy. I shivered, even though the sun had just risen and the day was already hot. I was frightened, but I didn't know why. Was it because my father looked so small compared to the soldiers? They were all so tall! I wondered if all Sudani people were this tall. Their skin was beautiful—it was black as night. I would have loved to touch it. Did it feel like my own skin?

My father beckoned to us and we moved toward him, huddled together in a small group. Lewteh was frightened. Her hand gripped mine tightly as the soldiers motioned us forward with quick movements of their rifles.

We made our way to a flatbed truck filled with other refugees. I wondered if they were Jews like us. I didn't think so. They were very dark, like the soldiers. When the truck pulled away from the border and drove along a dirt path, clouds of dust fanned out and covered all of us. One of the men spoke to my father in a language I'd never heard before, and my father raised his hands helplessly, asking, "Amharinya—do you speak Amharic?" The man shook his head no.

About an hour later, we reached a place that looked like a large army camp. There were rows and rows of square tents lined up as far as you could see. When we came to a stop in front of a small building, I made out a sign with the English letters S U F U W A.

Once inside, a foreigner wrote down all our names. My father learned that his younger brother, Alemu, was living in the camp and that Daniel's brother, Melessa, was also here, along with Daniel's two sons. When my father told the family about Daniel's death, his voice broke. "I feel responsible," he confessed. "I should have mounted a watch during the night."

After leaving Daniel's family with Melessa, we found my uncle Alemu in another part of the camp. He and his family had lived far from Dibebehar so I'd never met him before.

He greeted my father excitedly and then turned to welcome each one of us. "Thank God you have all survived," he said over and over, kissing us repeatedly and asking for our names. I watched him curiously. He looked just like my father except that he was even shorter and nearly bald, while my father still had quite a lot of hair.

"Come," he said, taking us to an empty tent right next to his. "When people left this tent last night, I was so happy. I just knew it was a sign that you would be here soon!"

The ground inside the tent was littered with stones and brambles so we tied some branches together and swept everything clean. Then, because there were no mattresses, we laid out all our spare clothing on the bare ground. For the first time in my life, my mother and I would be sleeping in the same place as my father and stepmother and the girls. As we arranged our things I couldn't help wondering whether it would be awkward for my mother, but if it was she showed no sign of it.

That first evening, we gathered around a small fire outside Alemu's tent to hear him speak about life in the camp. "The food here is very bad," he began. "The flour they give out is different from our *tef*. And the oil has a strange taste, like fish that's gone bad."

Alemu lowered his voice. "Some of our people refuse to eat the food because it isn't kosher. But I believe that we must eat what we are given. We need to keep up our strength. Many have sickened and died here, and, with God's help, I'm not going to let that happen to my family!"

"Try not to drink the water that comes from the pipes," Alemu warned. "It's dirty and we think that's why so many of our people have died. There's a stream not too far away. As long as you have the strength, go there for your water."

"What happens when someone dies here?" my father asked soberly.

"We bury them secretly, in the dark, outside of the camp. We try to go as far away as we can. Since there are no crosses on our graves, people can tell that we're Jews," Alemu answered.

When I heard that, I prayed that poor Daniel would be the only one of us to die before reaching Yerusalem.

"Come closer," Alemu whispered. We all leaned in toward him. "There are people in the camp from the Comitey."

"What is that?" my father whispered too.

"People who were sent from Yerusalem," Alemu answered. "But the Sudani must never know that they're here or they'll be killed."

We all nodded soberly. We would keep the secret.

"They come and write our names on a waiting list," Alemu explained, "and every month they give us money. If you get sick, they'll bring you medicine. When your turn comes, they'll take you out of the camp and fly you to Israel. But it might take a long time because many are waiting."

"God willing, may it be soon," my father said, mumbling a prayer.

And so, we waited. The days were hot and the nights were freezing. There were thousands of refugees in the camp and the lines for food and water were long. Most of the other people were Ethiopian Christians or Muslims who had come because of the war or the famine. Every day more people arrived, looking near death. Some were young men who wore tattered uniforms—they'd run away from the army. If they'd been caught, they would have been shot, for sure.

The first few nights, I lay awake listening to the sound of men's voices, sometimes singing and laughing and sometimes shouting in anger. There was beer sold in a tent near ours, and from the sound of it there were people inside who had drunk a lot of *tela*. People got into arguments at all hours of the night. Sometimes I heard women crying out, as though in pain.

Only a few days after we arrived, I became ill. My stomach was so weak that I could barely hold myself upright. I could do little more than lie on my clothes and pray. Sometimes I had to be helped, shaking badly, to the common trench to relieve myself.

Everyone's spirits were low. We'd come to Sudan with such high hopes and now we could do nothing but wait. Even though we'd been warned, I'd been sure that once we crossed the border we would be immediately spirited away to Yerusalem. But the man from the Comitey told us that some people had been waiting for more than two years! I prayed every night that this wouldn't happen to us.

My father and Alemu stood in line for our food and water and held secret discussions with the people from the Comitey. We girls were told to stay together and never leave the area just outside the tent. So apart from helping my mother and stepmother with the cooking and washing, there was very little for us to do. The girls and I passed the time sitting near the doorway, watching the people coming and going outside the tent.

Two little girls, twins named Fatima and Farida, lived in a tent near us. They were about the same age as Lewteh. We didn't know their language so we couldn't speak to them, and I knew that my father didn't want us to mingle with anyone who wasn't Beta Israel. But I liked to watch the twins play with a ball they'd made out of pieces of cloth. Watching them was something to do during the long, hot days.

One morning I was sitting on the ground outside our tent. I hadn't slept well. All night I'd heard the sounds of a woman crying. I was waiting for the girls to come out of their tent. It was late, but there was no sign of them.

Suddenly, there was a loud wailing coming from inside their tent. The screams were terrible. The twins' mother rushed out of the tent and began to run frantically in circles. She kept shaking her head and saying something over and over. I couldn't understand what she was saying. But I thought from the wailing that someone must have died. I prayed that it wasn't the twins.

"What happened?" Lewteh asked sleepily. She was sleeping later and later these days, whether from boredom or illness I wasn't sure.

"I think someone died in the twins' tent," I whispered. Lewteh's eyes were huge and I knew that she was thinking the same thing I was—please let it not be the two little girls!

But our prayers did no good. The wailing went on and on. I crouched close to the doorway and although our mothers tried to shield us, I caught sight of two small parcels, wrapped up in the twins' brightly colored scarves, being carried out of their tent in a solemn funeral procession.

"What did they die of?" I asked my mother.

She didn't answer. Her smooth face was suddenly wrinkled, as though she had aged overnight. But I didn't need to hear her answer. It was the same disease that I had. It was dysentery that usually killed the children so quickly here. I felt my stomach clench in fear. Would I be the next one to die? I'd been going to the latrine much less in the last day or so. Surely I had survived the disease?

"I will not die before going to Yerusalem," I promised my mother as she kissed my cheeks and smoothed the shortest braids away from my forehead.

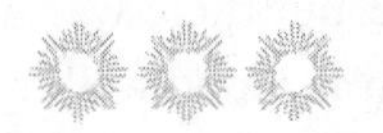

Weeks passed and the number of graves in the area surrounding the camp multiplied. Children and old people were the ones usually carried away for burial. Some were dying from disease, but most from hunger and from the polluted water.

We were more fortunate than many. We still had a bit of Dawid's money. Sometimes, when the rations were cut in half because of problems with transport, my father went to a nearby town. The food he brought back was purchased from the Saluki—Ethiopian merchants who had settled in the town. Their food came from over the border and was much better than what we were given in the camp. But when our money ran out, we'd be dependent on what the men from the Comitey managed to distribute.

One morning, we got up to find that Alemu and his family had disappeared! They were there when we all went to sleep, but in the morning they were gone—as though they'd never existed! How could that be?

"Where could they have gone?" my stepmother asked, shocked to find that their tent was empty. A few hours later, another family moved in where my uncle's family had been.

"Don't worry. The men from the Comitey must have taken them," my father whispered.

Our other neighbors were suspicious and kept asking where my uncle had gone. My father looked confident when he said that they had moved to another camp, that Alemu had been offered work. But I knew that their questions made him uneasy.

As for me, my uncle's disappearance renewed my flagging hopes. "You'll see, some day soon our neighbors will wake up and ask each other where we have gone," I whispered to Lewteh.

"*Inshallah*, if God wills it," she said.

I looked at her sharply. "Lewteh! You mustn't say the prayers of the Sudani people," I hissed. "We have our own prayers. Don't forget who you are!"

"I'm sorry, Wuditu," she answered sluggishly and I hugged her. Lately, she'd been so quiet. I'd noticed that she was moving around like an old woman—slowly and all bent over.

"Lewteh, why are you walking that way? Straighten up!" I said. She gave me a sad smile and straightened her back. But a moment later, she'd gone back to being bent over. I prayed that my sister wasn't getting sick. All around us people were dying. Every day funeral processions trailed out of the camp. Every day I asked God to keep my family safe.

A few days after Alemu had disappeared, a terrible thing happened. My father woke up to find that he couldn't see—both his eyes had swelled shut!

When my stepmother pulled his eyelids open with her fingers, he discovered that he could still see but poorly. We were afraid that he might go blind, but he didn't want to go to the camp doctor. "I don't want to draw attention to our family," he said.

"You have to see a doctor, Berihun," our mothers both urged. But my father refused to take a chance.

A few days later, a man from the Comitey came by. When he saw what had happened to my father, he promised to take him to Israel that very same night.

At first, my father refused to go. "I can't leave my family here," he protested. "Who will watch over them?"

"If you stay here much longer without medical help, you'll go blind," the man argued. "What use will you be to your family when that happens? In Israel, you'll get well. I promise to take the rest of your family on the very next flight. Come on now, there's no time, we have to hurry," he urged, pulling at my father's elbow. Finally, reluctantly, my father turned to follow him.

"Wait! He'll need someone to take care of him on the journey," my mother cried out. "Melkeh, you must go with him." But Father, knowing that Melkeh was the strong one, decided that my mother should go with him. Melkeh must stay and watch over the rest of us.

And so, in an instant, they were gone. I had only a moment to hug my mother and to touch my father's arm as they led him away. My mother looked back at me—one harried, sorrowful glance. There was silence after they left the tent. What had just happened? In an instant I had lost my mother and my father. I was too shocked to cry.

Melkeh was now the head of the family, but she—usually so strong and capable—was weeping, and although she quickly wiped her tears and gathered my sisters and I for a comforting hug, we all knew that she was no substitute for my father. He was the head of the family, the one who dealt with the men from the Comitey and the camp officials. He had always been the one who made the decisions and we had followed his lead.

Who would decide for us now that he was gone? Who would go to town for food when we were hungry? Who would stand in line for water? It was dangerous for girls to stand in line. Girls vanished when they had no man to protect them, and even Lewteh and I knew that those girls were taken as wives, sometimes even sold across the border. Who would keep us safe now that Father was gone?

That same night, the man from the Comitey came back, but it wasn't to take us away. Instead he told my stepmother to move two of our family into a tent that had just been vacated. "We've got to make it look like no one has left the camp," he said. When Melkeh protested that there were only girls in our family now, he added, "You must do as I say. The police are already suspicious of us. If they find an empty tent, they'll realize that there's been an airlift and they'll come to investigate. So—which two do you want to send?"

We all looked to Melkeh to make the decision. But she didn't seem able to decide. "If only Berihun were here," she said, wringing her hands in despair. "I don't know what to do!"

"Hurry up! I can't stay long," the man said impatiently. "Do you want me to choose?"

"No! No, I'll do it," she said worriedly. "There are only five of you now and Mulu'alem is much too young to go..."

She looked at Wubalu and Aster, the oldest and prettiest among us, and I could tell that she didn't want to bring the man's attention to them. My stepmother wouldn't want to put the girls in a separate tent and have them be grabbed by one of the men in the camp. That left only Lewteh and me to be sent to the other tent. I held my breath and waited to see what she would say next.

"If Maru goes along with them, it should be safe enough for Wuditu and Lewteh," she said, referring to a cousin who had recently arrived in the camp. He was 16, three years older than me and big for his age.

That night, I lay in the dark, listening to the sounds of men drinking and fighting in the nearby *tela beit*. With my father gone, the voices from the beer hall seemed so much more threatening and the night so much longer.

Don't be such a baby, I told myself, snuggling closer to Lewteh and trying to ignore Maru's loud snoring. Soon we'll all be safe.

Maru, Lewteh, and I spent our days and nights in the new tent, except for meals, which we shared with my stepmother and the girls. But on the third night, the man from the Comitey had still not come back for us and Maru had gotten sick. When the next night his fever was even higher and he began to moan loudly, I knew that I had to send him to Melkeh's tent.

"Melkeh told me to look after you and Lewteh! I can't leave you all by yourselves!" he protested, but I told him, "Go, Maru—go to Melkeh. We'll be okay. Don't worry about us."

Chapter 10

The refugee camp, later that night

Craack!

I woke instantly, and as the sound rang out again, I recognized it as rifle fire. Beside me, Lewteh sat up and clutched my arm. My throat, already parched and swollen from the dust and dry air, convulsed painfully. The shooting stopped, replaced by angry shouts and cries of fear.

"Shush, Lewteh, be quiet!" I whispered and pushed her behind me, cautiously peering out of our tent.

Dust, kicked up by hundreds of scrambling feet, billowed upward in the dim lights of the camp. But I could still make out the sight of soldiers dragging people from their tents and shoving them into the backs of trucks.

"No time to waste!" the soldiers yelled. "Come on! We're taking you to Israel!" I stood frozen in full view, too scared to move.

Two soldiers burst into our tent. Lewteh screamed in terror, but I managed to grab our bag of sugar and our nearly empty water can—the only rations we had left—before the soldiers picked us up and flung us into the back of a crowded truck.

I struggled to sit up, holding Lewteh tightly in my lap, as more and more people tumbled into the truck. An old man fell against me when someone tripped over him. His elbow dug into my side, making my already weakened stomach cramp painfully.

Just when I thought that I would give way to panic if any more people came aboard, the soldiers slammed the wooden barrier shut and our truck began to move. More trucks followed behind us and I could hear their passengers crying out as we moved out of the camp and rattled onto a dirt road.

Lewteh and I looked fearfully at each other. "Mother and the girls are still back there, Wuditu! How will we ever see them again?"

My mind struggled to make sense of what was happening. This wasn't the way people went to Yerusalem. It was supposed to be a secret. Yet all this was happening out in the open, with a lot of noise. And the people who were taking us couldn't be from the Comitey. They were wearing uniforms.

"Do you think the soldiers will really take us to Yerusalem?" I asked the people around me.

"That's what they say," a man answered. But I could tell he didn't believe it.

The line of trucks drove all through the night, and I held Lewteh close to me on the bouncing flatbed. She slept sweetly as she always did, her little nose wrinkling up and her body heavy and warm against mine. Sometimes I nodded off, my head drooping over my sister. But then I would wake again with a start.

After long hours, a faint light appeared on the horizon and people scrambled to their feet to see where we were.

"We're going the wrong way! This is the way back to the Ethiopian border!" a woman near me cried out.

"Yxaviher, give me strength," I prayed as the trucks screeched to a sudden stop.

The soldiers flung open the wooden gate and gestured silently with their weapons for us to climb down. Holding tightly on to Lewteh, I moved on cramped, wobbly legs and peered about. There was nothing to see but hard, cracked earth and an occasional low bush, too low even for shelter from the sun, which was already beginning to beat down on us.

I watched as refugees from more than a dozen trucks were herded together. One of the soldiers scooped up a handful of dirt and raised his arm in the air. Then he grabbed a woman near me by the arm and began shoveling dirt into her mouth, as we all looked on in shock.

"You Ethiopians, do you see this dirt? This is our dirt, our land—not yours!" he shouted as he scooped up more and more handfuls of dirt, cramming them into the poor woman's mouth. She stumbled and fell, her legs splayed on the ground, her upper body held fast by the soldier's grip on her arm. I stared at her gaping, dirt-filled mouth, hardly able to believe what I was seeing. Had he killed her? No. Her eyes were still moving!

"We've allowed you to stay as guests in our country and you've betrayed us," he said, dropping the woman carelessly onto the ground.

She gagged and coughed and tried to spit out the dirt. She choked terribly, and finally, no longer able to bear her suffering and with Lewteh tagging desperately behind me, I crept up to her. To my relief, the soldier turned his back on us and I knelt and carefully poured water from my water can into her mouth.

"Your country is in that direction!" the soldier continued, ignoring the woman weeping and coughing on the ground behind him. "Start walking back to Ethiopia right now! Anyone caught trying to sneak back to our country will be shot! Do as we say and no one will get hurt!"

Before anyone had a chance to say anything, the soldiers climbed into the trucks, slammed the doors shut, and sped back in the direction of the refugee camp. We remained as we were for several seconds. No one spoke or moved. Gradually, people began to come back to life. Some cried, some were sick, and others stretched their cramped legs and stared blankly toward the Ethiopian border.

As people began to move toward the border, Lewteh wept quietly and I put my arms around her.

"What should we do now, Wuditu?" Lewteh sobbed.

"Just a minute, Lewteh, I'm trying to decide!"

I looked around me. There was nothing to see but vast wilderness and scattering refugees. One or two men were sneaking back toward the camp. But they were moving fast, too fast for us to catch them. If we tried to do the same, we'd have to do it alone. For just a minute, I considered it. How I longed to take a chance. If only we could get back to Melkeh and the girls!

But then I looked at Lewteh. Her life depended on

my decision. Even if we were lucky and the soldiers didn't catch us, how would I find the way? No. Our best chance for staying alive was to stick with the other refugees.

"Hurry—we mustn't fall behind!" I hissed, pulling Lewteh by the hand.

Chapter 11

En route to Ethiopia, 1989

Wuditu, 13, and Lewteh, 10

I don't know how long it took us—it could have been two weeks or three. My memory of that time isn't clear, but I do remember that all through that first day, I'd struggled to keep moving over sand that burned my feet like coals of fire. In the scramble to leave, I'd left my shoes behind.

There were many people walking all around us, but none of them was my mother or my father, my aunt or my uncle. That first morning, some of the younger men had started running back toward the refugee camp. One of those young men was a cousin of ours. Ever since then, I'd been asking myself why I hadn't run after him and begged him to take us with him.

I felt that Lewteh knew my thoughts, and that she might blame me for this decision. But if she did, she never said anything.

I tried to put my anger and my fear aside and think about things that would keep us strong. "In Ethiopia we'll find relatives and they'll take care of us," I said.

"I don't know if I can walk that far, Wuditu," she answered listlessly.

"Of course you can," I said harshly. "Didn't you walk all the way to Sudan?" Lewteh didn't answer, but at least she kept on walking.

The days were hot and the nights were terribly cold. That first night, Lewteh and I cleared the area where we would sleep. We piled up a few smooth rocks to put under our heads, just as we did when we had slept in the fields at home. The sand was still warm, but the stones were already cold. We huddled together, shivering, but taking some comfort from the fact that there were adults nearby.

Sometime in the middle of the night I woke up to what sounded like the cries of a tiny kitten. But when I sat up, I saw that it wasn't an animal making that noise but Lewteh, sitting upright, with tears streaming down her cheeks.

"What's the matter?" I asked sleepily.

"I'm so cold, Wuditu. I can't stop shaking and my legs hurt so much!" she answered. I saw how badly she was shivering, but her forehead was cool. I murmured softly to her, wrapped my *netela* around us both, and drew her back down onto the ground.

"Go to sleep, Lewteh. In the morning, I'll rub your legs until they feel better," I promised. I was very worried about her. Lewteh hadn't been keeping up with the others. She was walking all hunched over. When I questioned her about it, she answered that her legs hurt. Lewteh was very brave. If she complained of pain and cried a lot, there had to be a reason for it. But what could it be? The idea that she might have some strange disease frightened me. And the knowledge that I was the one responsible for her now lay heavily on my heart.

That morning, an elderly man had collapsed near us, saying, "I can't go any farther." His daughter and grandchild had looked silently at the rest of us and we'd all stopped for a brief rest. But the sun scorched us and we had no water. We had to keep moving.

"*Hiddoo, hiddoo*—go on ahead!" the old man urged his daughter. "Take the young ones and go. I'll be fine. I just need to rest for a little while longer. Soon I'll get up and make my way slowly after you. I'll find you at the border."

Thinking of that old man, I worried about what would happen if Lewteh wouldn't be able to keep up. Would we, too, be left behind? I told myself, I'll carry Lewteh back to Ethiopia if I have to.

Exhausted, I fell back to sleep, groping around on the ground to make sure that our water can and our small bag of sugar hadn't been stolen during the night.

In the morning, I was startled awake by a man's loud cry. It was our cousin Melessa, Daniel's brother!

"Lewteh, Wuditu! Where's Berihun? Where's the rest of the family?" he asked.

"Back in the camp, I think," I answered. "Where's your family? Where are Daniel's wife and children and the two old aunties?"

"Still back there," he answered sadly. "When the soldiers came, I was out of the tent, waiting in line for our rations. They pointed their guns at me and I had no choice but to get into a truck."

I reached up and hugged him. He was just as big as Daniel—perhaps even taller. I was so relieved he'd found us that I burst into tears! The idea of walking all the way back to Ethiopia seemed less frightening now, with Melessa at our side.

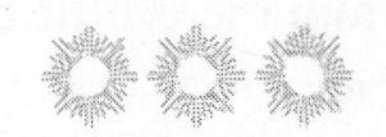

After all these years, I can't remember much more about the journey. I know that one night we were set upon by thieves. Our ration of sugar had long ago been consumed and our battered water can didn't seem to interest them. So Lewteh, Melessa, and I were left alone.

We were always hungry and thirsty; that I remember well. As the days passed and Lewteh's condition worsened, I grew more and more worried about her. I also wondered why the soldiers had taken us from the camp. What crime had we committed that we were thrown into the desert like garbage? I had no answers. I tried to hold on to the hope that we would find our family someday. I remember that I wanted to cry, but I knew that I must not. What would become of Lewteh if I gave way to tears?

Finally, we came to Tikil Dingay, a town on the Ethiopian side of the border. There, we were met by a man named Waga who had been sent by the Israelis to help us, and at last we were told the reason why we'd been banished from the refugee camp.

"The rebels who are fighting Mengistu used to have an agreement with Israel," Waga explained. "Whenever they could, the rebels helped the Beta Israel on their way to

Sudan. But because so many people were dying there, Israel wanted to find a safer route. So they made a new alliance with Mengistu and persuaded him to let the Beta Israel fly to Israel directly from Ethiopia. Now, thousands of Jews have left their villages and gone to Addis Ababa, to the Israeli embassy. From there, little by little, people have started getting to Israel.

"But as for the rebels," Waga went on, "they felt betrayed by Israel and decided to take revenge on the Jews in the refugee camps. That's the reason why you were all thrown out of Sudan—the rebels incited the Sudani soldiers to do it. You weren't the only ones this happened to—hundreds of people were expelled that day!"

Lewteh and I were exhausted and I'd been discouraged, thinking that we might still have to walk all the way back to Sudan in order to get to Yerusalem. But from what Waga said, it seemed that we might be able to get there from Addis Ababa!

"Now that you've all made it back to Ethiopia, everything will be all right," Waga reassured us. "Eat and drink and get some rest and in a day or two we'll take you back to your villages."

"Why can't you take us to Addis?" Melessa asked. That's what we were all thinking.

"No. It would be too dangerous to move so many people at once. The soldiers would surely stop us and arrest us. You have to go back to the villages. But don't worry. Once you get there, you'll find people who've been sent to take you to Addis," he answered.

Waga handed out small amounts of money and sacks

of flour to everyone, including Lewteh and me. We were exhausted and if we hadn't been so hungry, we might have fallen asleep the moment we arrived. Instead, Lewteh and Melessa waited impatiently while I cooked a small amount of *injera*. Little though it was, it seemed like a feast to us. We ate and drank until our stomachs were bursting and then fell asleep on the floor of an abandoned schoolhouse. Lewteh and I slept facing each other, curled protectively around our water can, our money, and our ration of flour. For the first time since we had been taken from the refugee camp, I relaxed and slept soundly.

The next morning, Melessa asked to be taken to Amba Giorgis, a large market town named after the Christianos' Saint George that was two days' walk from Dibebehar. Lewteh and I waited for him to tell us to go with him, but that didn't happen. He acted as though we weren't even related to him! So when he began to climb onto one of the buses, I grabbed his arm and said, "Aren't we coming with you?"

"*Chigger yelem*, no problem," he answered with a shrug.

We drove through the villages, stopping several times to let people off. Melessa directed the driver to leave us near a grassy hill on the outskirts of Amba Giorgis. "It'll be dark soon," he said thoughtfully. "I'll go into town and find us a place to sleep. Wait here and I'll come back for you as soon as I can."

We waited on the grass for hours. "Do you think Cousin Melessa will come back soon?" Lewteh asked over and over. Night had fallen and we were shivering. Lewteh was coughing badly and I was worried that bandits might hear her and attack us before Melessa came back. Bandits or worse—hyenas!

Somewhere not far from us, I could hear a pack of them, giggling shrilly. I hated that sound, for I knew what it meant! Then I heard a small animal cry out and I shivered and looked around for something large and heavy to fight them off if they should come near us. There was nothing but a few rocks to throw at them.

Can I beat them off with my water can? I wondered grimly. That would have to do. I would not let the hyenas eat my sister.

"If we lie down in the tall grass, how will Cousin Melessa find us?" Lewteh asked, exhausted.

"We can shout out to him," I suggested.

"Not if we're sleeping, Wuditu," she answered, her eyes already nearly closed.

"Go to sleep, Lewteh. I'll look out for him," I said.

"When you get tired, wake me and I'll watch for him," she offered, but, listening to the hyenas, still giggling over their prey, I thought, If God gives me strength, I'll stay awake all night.

When morning came, we both woke up at the same time. "Why didn't you wake me?" Lewteh grumbled.

"I fell asleep," I admitted.

"Did Cousin Melessa come back?" she asked.

"I don't think so," I answered, looking around for him.

I heard a thin whinny to my left and turned, hoping to see Melessa. Perhaps he waited until the market was open to buy a horse to carry Lewteh.

It wasn't Melessa but a herd of wild ponies, moving in and out of the mist.

"Look!" I nudged Lewteh, and she laughed and

clapped her hands. It was the first sign of pleasure I'd seen on her face since we'd been turned out into the desert. But her smile faded quickly. "What shall we do, Wuditu?" she asked. "We can't wait for Cousin Melessa forever. How could he leave us here? Do you think something bad happened to him?"

"He's not as nice as Cousin Daniel," I answered grimly, trying to think. There were several Beta Israel villages near Amba Giorgis. Senvetige was only a day's walk away and we had relatives there. Perhaps they would know how to make my sister well.

The trek to Senvetige took us two days—twice as long as it would have if Lewteh hadn't been so ill. I was carrying our water can and our ration of flour, and for the last hour or two I was practically carrying my sister. We rested often and I prayed a lot and begged God to give me the strength to get us safely to our destination.

But as we drew near, the village looked deserted. Where is everyone? I wondered. Then I remembered what Waga had said about people going to Addis. Had most of the Jews already left? If our relatives had gone, we'd come a long way for nothing.

As we walked through the village, we could see that there were still a few people living among the empty houses. Drawing near to Melkeh's uncle's house, we were relieved to find Kes Baruch and his wife. The elderly couple was still there, waiting for their granddaughter to give birth before setting out for Addis.

Kes Baruch told us that some of his people had gone to Amba Giorgis and never come back. "A *faranj* from

America met them there and took them to Addis Ababa," he said. "From there they went to Yerusalem."

"That's just what Waga told us in Tikil Dingay!" I said to Lewteh. "I wonder if Melessa met that *faranj* and that's why he never came back." I didn't want to believe that Daniel's brother would leave us without a good reason.

That first few days, I was so tired. But after I'd rested, I began to think about what to do next. Lewteh wasn't getting any better. God forbid it—but what if she got worse? There were people out there who were taking the Beta Israel to Addis, but it seemed that we had to find them first.

"I've decided to go to Amba Giorgis," I told Lewteh. I'd never been alone before and I was scared. But I knew that my sister wouldn't be able to come with me. She'd barely made it to Senvetige. And even if she could walk that far, it might take me a while to find those *faranj*. How would I pay for food and lodging for the two of us until then?

"Don't leave me alone here, Wuditu," she begged and began to cry loudly.

"Shh! Lewteh, stop crying. Listen. I'm not leaving you alone. Kes Baruch and his family will look after you. Those *faranj* who are taking people to Addis—they'll never find us in this tiny village," I said, trying to make her understand. "I'll have to go and look for them. And when I do, I'll come back for you. We'll go together to Yerusalem—wouldn't you like that?"

"Don't go, Wuditu," Lewteh pleaded. "I'm afraid something bad will happen to you."

"Don't be silly. Nothing will happen to me," I promised. I knelt down beside her, taking her chin in my hand and wiping away her tears. I kissed her good-bye on both cheeks and pressed her back down onto her pallet.

"Be good, *chakla*. I'll see you very soon," I said.

"God be with you," she mumbled and then her eyes closed and she lay still.

Yxaviher, please don't let my sister die! I prayed silently. I watched her sleep for a while before turning to go.

As I was leaving, Kes Baruch came to say good-bye. "I made these for you," he said, handing me a pair of shoes. "They're very strong, see? I cut out a piece from an inner tire and fastened it to the bottom of the shoes. So even if your path is full of thorns—and I pray that it won't be—the tire will stop you from getting holes in your shoes."

As he handed them to me, I could feel the old man's arms trembling. "May your journey be an easy one," he said, "and may you walk in these shoes for many years to come!"

They were the best pair of shoes I ever had. I was touched that such a holy man would bother to make them for me.

"You are as strong as these shoes that I've made for you, Wuditu," he said, kissing me repeatedly on my cheeks. "I pray that you will find that *faranj*. And when you do, don't forget to come back for us!"

Part Three

The Tela Beit

CHAPTER 12

Amba Giorgis, 1989

Wuditu, 13

When I left my sister, I knew that it might take me a while to get back to her. Until then, I thought that I could earn my keep by working as a servant in someone's house. In my spare time, I would look for the foreigners that Waga and Kes Baruch had talked about.

That was my plan. But I had very little money and no experience of town ways, and after a few days in Amba Giorgis, I realized that finding work and a place to stay would be much harder than I'd imagined. Because of the war, people were pouring into town from areas where fighting was taking place, and the local people were afraid to take strangers into their homes for fear of being robbed. The first person I asked for work said to me, "I'll hire you, but only if you bring me a reference."

I was stumped. Of course, there was no one I could ask for a reference. So I tried to think of what I would say to the next person who asked me for one. "I've run away from my village, from a cruel husband," I told everyone I met. "I didn't realize that I had to have a reference. Do you know anyone who needs a servant? I'm a very hard worker."

Often, I was asked if I was a good Christian girl and I always said that I was. I didn't like having to lie, but I knew that I had to be very careful not to let anyone find out that I was Beta Israel. I'd already seen that the people in town hated and feared us as much as the ones in the village had. Sadly, even lying about my faith didn't help me get a job.

Living in town was very expensive. A piece of *injera* bread cost ten centimes and was hardly enough to keep my belly full. I'd located a woman named Almaz, who was the owner of a *tela beit*—a beer house. She rented pallets for the night on her living room floor for fifty centimes. So it cost me nearly a whole birr a day to live in town! The money Waga had given me ran out within a few days, and I'd seen no sign of any foreigners. I was starting to be very worried.

There were a lot of soldiers in town, and as I wandered the alleyways looking for work I was often harassed. It wasn't safe for me to be out alone like this, but I wasn't willing to give up and go back to Senvetige. My great fear was that if I went back before finding help, my sister might die. But I couldn't allow myself to have these thoughts. Whatever happened, I would keep searching until I was successful.

Since I couldn't find work as a servant, I began to support myself by carrying water for people in the town. It was either that or taking flour to the mill—a task that took longer and paid less. Carrying water all day was hard work, but as time passed, I began to feel proud that I was managing to keep myself clean and fed. I felt strong and independent.

But I worried constantly about Lewteh. How was she? What if she'd gotten worse? What if she had died while I was here, trying to find help for us? Whenever I had these thoughts, I told myself, I've left her in good hands. Kes Baruch is a man of God, a fine man who wouldn't just let my sister die.

So I stayed on. But it was difficult to look for the foreigners when I had to carry water all day. I listened to the conversations of the other water carriers and I kept my ears open for gossip in the market. But I never heard anything that might help solve our problem.

One evening, I overheard people in the market talking about the *falashas*.

"Have you heard?" a young soldier said. "All the *falashas* have been taken from the villages. They've completely disappeared—there's not a single one left!"

"Really? What happened to them—did someone kill them all?" A woman laughed.

"No," he laughed too. "They all went to Addis Ababa," he said.

"Why?"

"I heard that they're all being sent to Israel," the soldier replied. "Nobody wants them here."

"Better for us!" Another man spat on the ground, and others nodded. "Now we won't have to be afraid of their evil eye," he said, and the others murmured their agreement.

I smiled along with them, as though this news meant nothing to me. But my whole body was shaking and I looked desperately for a place to be alone. Behind a row of houses, I sank down onto the ground and wept in sorrow and fear.

Why did I leave the village when I did? Why didn't I stay just a bit longer? All this time I'd been looking in the wrong place. And now I was alone. I couldn't understand why Kes Baruch or Lewteh hadn't sent someone for me—might someone still come?

After a while, I started to pray. I prayed that Lewteh was on her way to Israel. I prayed that my parents had gotten there too. If Lewteh would only tell my father where I was, he might come for me. But then I thought, Father is old and nearly blind. How can he come all the way from Yerusalem to look for me?

I thought of my brother but quickly realized that Dawid had important work to do, for Israel and for my people. Who knew if he'd be able to leave his work to come and look for his sister? Who knew if he was safe? He might have been caught during his travels in Ethiopia—he might even be in jail!

I thought, I'm like a dead person. Only a dead person has no one to sustain them and nothing to hope for, not even something to pray for! It would have been better if God had made me a Christian or a Muslim. Even a pagan would have been better. Why did he make me a Jew? So that I would suffer alone and die alone?

I looked around, afraid that I might have spoken my thoughts out loud. Where did they come from? If I hadn't been born a Jew, I would never have known my beloved family. I thought of my mother. What would she say? She would tell me that giraffes never cry, I thought wryly. She would tell me to stand up straight and calm myself and think of a new plan.

So be it, I thought. I'm alone and there's no one to help me. Never mind! I'm alive and I'm strong. Somehow, I'll find more work and I'll save money and I'll buy a bus ticket to Addis Ababa and then I'll get to Yerusalem by myself! And no one will ever know what terrible thoughts I've had today!

Then I had another idea. There was a kiosk in town, made of dung and mud, and a girl—not too much older than me—who sat there all day and wrote letters for people. This was how she made her living. As I passed on my way to and from the water pumps, I often thought that if I'd had time to finish my schooling I might have been able to do the same thing. That would surely have been easier than carrying water.

If I had enough money for paper, an envelope, and a stamp and to pay this girl, I could ask her to send a letter for me to Gojjam. My father's oldest brother, Yonah, lived there. Before we left for Sudan, my father had begged his brother to come with us. "The time is now," he had written to him. But Yonah refused to come with us. He'd gone to school and become a teacher and married a non-Jewish woman, a teacher like him. They lived a good life. "We'll come later," he wrote back.

Now I realized that I could write to my uncle in Gojjam. If he got a letter from me he would surely help me. And if not, I could still save for a bus ticket. It would take longer, but it was good to have two plans, not just one.

Exhausted but a little more hopeful, I went to sleep that night in my usual place. I felt safe there because, although Almaz sometimes took a customer into her bed after the *tela beit* closed, I'd never seen other men sleeping in her living room, only women.

But this time, there was a group of soldiers on leave and it smelled like they'd drunk a lot of *tela*. I should go, I thought. But the men were asleep and I'd already paid Almaz for the night. So I moved my pallet as far away from them as I could get. I listened to them snoring for a while and then I went to sleep.

I woke up in the dark to a strong smell of *tela*, right up against my face! I felt someone kneeling over me and then a hand searching my clothes. I heard the sound of cloth ripping. Before I could move or say anything, a man pinned my hands to the floor. He slumped down on top of me and I was shocked to feel his bare legs on mine! I felt his teeth pulling at the neck of my *kemis*! "Come on, help me!" he whispered.

I lay stiff and still. I didn't know what to do! The room was full of armed soldiers. What would they do to me if they woke up? Would it be better to scream or to keep quiet?

I lay pinned. My wrists hurt from the pulling of his fists. His weight shifted for a moment and I tried to kick him. But he was heavy and I was afraid.

Suddenly, his legs began to force mine open and I finally found the strength to move. I screamed and kicked and rocked my body from side to side. The soldier cursed and fought to hold me down.

"Shush, don't make any noise, I'll give you money," he coaxed. I continued to thrash around and scream until the men around us began to wake up and complain.

"*Ishi, ishi*, all right," he muttered and rolled off me and onto his back. I paid careful attention to the sounds he was making, praying that when he had satisfied himself he would go to sleep. Then I sat up and wrapped my torn *kemis* around my legs. I leaned my back against the wall of the *tela beit* and tried to calm my breathing. I breathed in and out, concentrating until my breathing made hardly any sound. I knew that it was important to be quiet.

I must have fallen over in the night because when I woke up I found that I was lying on the floor near my pallet. The soldiers were gone, and Almaz was shaking my shoulder and telling me to get up so that she could sweep the floor.

She gave me a needle and thread to fix my torn *kemis*. "Why did you refuse him?" she asked. "These soldiers have plenty of money in their pockets. They would have paid you well." I kept quiet, but I knew that I had to leave this place at once and find another way to save myself.

That morning, instead of asking the girl in the kiosk how much it would cost to write a letter, I used my last few birr to take the bus to Gondar City. If there were any Beta Israel left and they were trying to get to Addis Ababa, they would most likely go through the bus station in the provincial capital—that's where I'd have the best chance of finding help. Besides, whatever happened there, it couldn't be worse than staying here.

I could only hope that I wasn't too late.

Chapter 13

The bus to Gondar City, 1990

Wuditu, 14

I was bruised and sore from struggling with the soldier, and every bounce along the road from Amba Giorgis to Gondar City caused me pain. I wanted to sleep and forget the terror of the night before, but I couldn't stop thinking about what had happened.

The woman in the seat next to me put an end to my thoughts by poking me in the side. "What are you doing, going to Gondar City all by yourself at a time like this?" she asked. "Didn't you hear? There's fighting in the city. If I didn't have a husband and children there I wouldn't go back myself."

"I'm looking for work as a servant," I told her. "Do you know anyone who might give me a job?"

"Do you have any references?" the woman asked, looking at my worn clothing.

"No," I answered. I gave her the same reply I'd given to the people in Amba Giorgis, but with a few new details that I'd added over the last few days. "I've run away from my husband. He beat me every day and I just couldn't stand it any longer. When I fled, I was too frightened to think about bringing a reference. But I'm a very good worker," I said, bowing my head.

The woman turned to look out the bus window. She craned her neck, staring at something. I was hurt. She hadn't even bothered to answer me. Her loud sniff and rigid back made it clear what she thought. A girl dressed in rags and with no one to vouch for her—who would hire her?

I looked past her, trying to see what it was that had made her stare so intently. I saw an enormous pile of confiscated weapons being guarded by rebel soldiers. Not an unusual sight—I wondered that she stared so hard. Unlike the government army, the rebel forces had girl and boy soldiers. I watched as the girls paced proudly, with their weapons in their arms. They looked so sure and strong! I envied them their fearlessness!

The woman turned back to me and said, "I would like to help you, dear, but I don't know anyone who needs a servant. This is not a good time for a young girl to be alone in the city. Be careful."

"Yes, you're right," I answered. Her tone was caring, and before I could think if it was the right thing to do, I had confided in her about what had nearly happened to me the night before.

"So many years of war, so many soldiers—you're just another victim to them," she said, shaking her head. "It might be safer for you, in spite of everything, to go back to your husband."

"I will not go back," I said firmly. I felt bad about lying to such a nice woman. I longed to tell her the truth. My lies and my loneliness had become such heavy burdens. But the truth was too dangerous to reveal.

"Are you from the city?" I asked.

"I was born in Debark," she answered. "I just came back from visiting my sister there. I was only going to be there for a few days, but when I saw what was happening I stayed on to help those poor, poor people."

"What poor people?" I asked. I had no idea what she was talking about.

"Don't you know? There is famine in the north and the K'ai Maskal, the Red Cross, has a feeding station in Debark. Hundreds—no thousands—of people have come looking for food. It's terrible how they look, wasted and with bellies swollen with hunger. The babies are the worst. Their faces are like people already dead. There's barely any flesh on their poor little bones."

"How can this be? I've heard nothing of this," I murmured in shock. Debark was only a few miles from Amba Giorgis. How could we not have heard what was happening?

"It's true. I also knew nothing of this until I got there," the woman went on. "Mengistu's government doesn't want anyone to know what is happening. My sister only knows about it because she lives there. She's been helping to feed the refugees so I stayed to help too."

She lowered her voice and said, "When I was young, I wasn't always such a good person and my conscience has been bothering me. Two years ago one of my daughters was bitten by a dog and died of rabies. I nearly went crazy.

I was sure it was a punishment for the wrongdoing of my youth. I mourned for a long time. And then my husband said, 'Go spend some time with your sister. Perhaps a change of place will help you to overcome your sorrow.'"

"And did it?" I asked.

"Yes, very much so," she answered. "Seeing those poor people showed me that I am actually a very fortunate woman. I still have other healthy children." The woman mumbled a prayer to protect her children. "And there are people in this world who are more unfortunate than I am. I've prayed about it and now I see that I can protect my loved ones and give my life meaning by helping people in the future."

After that, we talked about less important matters. I kept wondering if this nice woman would help me if she knew my real situation. But fear kept me silent. I was a liar and a Jew. How could she treat me with anything but contempt if I revealed my secrets?

When the bus pulled into Gondar City, the woman gathered her things together. "Good-bye," she said kindly and wished me luck.

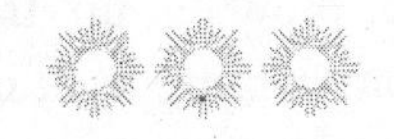

I'd never been alone in a big city before. I was scared and I prayed that I had done the right thing in using the last of my money to come here. At first, I stayed close to the bus station. I was looking for a foreigner—an American, I'd been told. But I didn't see any *faranj* among the crowds and after a while, my confidence grew and I began to move farther away from the station.

As I walked, I came across a crowd of people. They were watching a group of government soldiers being marched off to jail by rebel soldiers. The crowd was spitting and throwing stones at the prisoners.

"Down with Mengistu!" one man shouted.

"Death to the Butcher of Addis!" another screamed. The rebel soldiers struggled to keep the crowd away from the prisoners.

"These are nothing but young boys," a man next to me said, shaking his head. "They were probably taken from their village in a government raid. Now, suddenly, they're the enemy!" I nodded and continued to move forward.

Boom! Boom! Boom!

Without any warning, three large blasts rocked the area. I cringed when a block of wood fell off a building and landed only a few meters from where I was standing.

I was bent over, coughing from the dust kicked up by the blasts, when I heard loud, high shrieks. "What happened?" a woman screamed, running out of a building and hugging a child to her breast.

"The rebels are blowing up the bridges to stop Mengistu's tanks from coming back into the city," someone answered.

"Oh, my God—look at that, look at that!" another woman cried and people rushed forward to see.

I pushed my way to the front of the crowd and was stunned to see two eyes staring up at me! I stood completely still, trying to make sense of what I was seeing. It was a man's head, lying right there on the roadside! I gagged and turned away, pushing blindly outward while the crowd continued to stand there, muttering uneasily.

I ran back to the bus station and leaned against an inner wall, trying to catch my breath.

What do I do now? I thought. That woman on the bus was right. I shouldn't be here. How stupid I was to think I could just walk around and find a *faranj* to save me!

I realized that with all this fighting, people would be suspicious of strangers, just like in Amba Giorgis. I would never find work here. At least in Amba Giorgis people knew me a little. They'd seen me carrying water all over town. One of my customers might even hire me. Then I wouldn't have to be afraid—I'd have a safe place to sleep.

Whatever my decision, I needed to make it quickly. It would be dark in another few hours, too dark to walk all the way back to Amba Giorgis. And I couldn't stay in the city—I had no money for a bed.

I tried to think past the tiredness, hunger, and fear. I looked around, wondering if I might be able to sneak onto a bus. But it seemed hopeless. There were huge crowds waiting for every bus. How would I be able to get past all those people and past the *zabanya* who was taking tickets? I caught sight of a flatbed truck parked next to the buses that were going to Amba Giorgis. I pushed my way through the crowd and struggled to climb up onto the back of the truck.

I must have passed out after that because I don't remember the ride or how I got off the truck. It was dark when I found myself at Almaz's door. The lights were off so I sank down onto a rock by her front door and fell asleep.

I woke up to hear Almaz shouting, "Aiee, Wuditu! Why are you sleeping out here?"

"I'm so tired, but I don't have any more money," I said weakly, nearly in tears. "May I please stay the night?" I pleaded. "If you'll let me sleep here, I'll carry water for you tomorrow."

Muttering and cursing, Almaz opened the door and pointed to her living room floor, which, thank God, was empty. "You can sleep on the floor again tonight, but I can't let you stay without paying any longer than that," she said firmly.

The next morning, I left early to fetch water. My sleep had been disturbed by terrible dreams and I was weak with hunger and thirst. When I returned from the water pumps, Almaz looked me over carefully, then told me to come and share her breakfast. When I hesitated, she said, "*Chigger yelem*, no problem. You said you were looking for work?"

I nodded.

"My daughter recently married and moved away," she said. "Now I don't have anyone to help me brew *tela* for my customers."

She gave me another sharp glance and then asked, "Are you a good Christian girl, honest and hard-working?"

I bowed and nodded and the deal was struck.

Chapter 14

Amba Giorgis, 1990

Wuditu, 14

I tried not to let her see it, but I was trembling badly while I explained my conditions to Almaz.

"I will not work as a prostitute, only as a servant," I told her. "I'll earn my living by doing all the housework and by brewing *tela*. If you agree, I'll put my sleeping mat on the back porch, well away from the living room. And I won't serve the customers or sleep with them."

I was taking a big risk in trying to set terms with her. What if she changed her mind about hiring me?

"*Ishi*, all right," she nodded, after a terrifyingly long minute of consideration.

It didn't take me very long to learn how things worked. Beer was brewed where I slept, in Almaz's back porch, and served to customers in her living room. People came to drink nearly every day but especially on Saturdays, when farmers coming back from the market and soldiers on leave would have a little money in their pockets. On those days, people drank much more freely.

Sometimes Almaz took a customer into her bed after she closed up for the night and often she'd hire other women for the same purpose. Most of the beer houses in Amba Giorgis increased their profits by hiring prostitutes.

My duties were heavy but less so than when I'd been on the streets carrying water. After the first few days, I began to feel calmer and my hopes for the future returned. I hoped that I could work for Almaz, be safe, and still look for a way to get back to my family.

Almaz's living room was a busy place. It was full of customers during the day, and at night the prostitutes would go to work. As time went on, I wondered how I could have been so ignorant as to think that I would be safe renting a pallet in her living room. God was looking after me, I thought, and rather than being upset at what had nearly happened, I came to see that I'd had a very lucky escape.

There were girls of the night that came often to the *tela beit*, and some that came only once or twice and then never again. I didn't let myself get close to any of them until I met China. I was always afraid that I would say something that would reveal the fact that I was a Jew. If people learned that I'd lied to them, I'd be in serious trouble. Anything could happen to me and there was no one to whom I could turn for protection.

But it was hard to resist China. She was only two or three years older than I was, and although her life had been harder than mine, she never seemed sad. We met during the rainy season. The farmers were busy planting some crops and harvesting others. With that and the rain, the men rarely came into town. It was a quiet time for Almaz and for China, but not for me because the housework went on no matter what time of year.

I'd given China this nickname because she had slanted eyes and an unusually pale, striking face. I tried not to stare at her, but sometimes I couldn't help myself. Her beauty gave me such pleasure. She was so tiny that her head didn't even reach my chin, and she had a huge smile that made you want to smile right back at her. She was always cheerful—the only complaint I ever heard her make was that her neck hurt from always having to look up at people, and even that was said with a smile.

You couldn't have found two women more different than Almaz and China. Where China was small-boned and delicate, Almaz was round and chunky. Our men like women to be fat as it is a sign of plenty. So even though Almaz was an older woman she had many admirers. She was very proud of her figure and flirted in a very girlish way with the customers. Sometimes, I was embarrassed for her. China, on the other hand, never flirted at all, although attracting men was her business.

China sometimes helped Almaz serve *tela*, but she wasn't a servant like me, she was a prostitute. The customers loved her and sometimes fights broke out over who would get to take her to bed. She preferred to work in a hotel, but if a customer didn't have enough money, she'd sometimes agree to stay with him in Almaz's living room.

I never saw China in the daytime. She slept most of the day. But I thought about her a lot while I worked. I'd wanted her to be my friend almost from the first moment

I saw her. In the village I would never have had a prostitute for a friend, but in town I was learning a different way of life. And when I heard China's story, I thought that she wasn't responsible for the way her life had turned out.

On days when there weren't any customers, China often brought a stool into the back porch and sat down beside me as I worked. One rainy day we'd been chatting about nothing in particular. China's fingers moved in quick circles as she spun cotton for a new *kemis*. The sound of the rain on the tin roof was nearly deafening, and suddenly her eyes began to have a mischievous look that I'd begun to recognize. A minute later, I watched as she got up and started dancing to the beat of the raindrops.

"Come dance with me, Wuditu," she invited and soon we were facing each other and moving our shoulders quickly up and down, forward and backward. The rain drummed in our ears and before we knew it, Almaz had joined us and the three of us were dancing the *eskesta*, the shoulder dance, clapping our hands and singing.

"Aiee! You two young ones carry on, I'm going to sleep!" Almaz gasped a few minutes later, her hands on her chest. "Don't forget to keep an eye on the *tela*, Wuditu!" she warned.

I nodded and China continued singing and dancing. Her eyes were closed and she seemed to be dreaming. I stood still and watched her graceful movements and a moment later she began to sing another song, one that was very popular. Each line of the chorus ended with the word *Lewteh*, and I felt a terrible pain in my heart as I listened to her. Where was my sister now? Would I ever see her again?

"Come, Wuditu, you're not dancing. Why have you stopped?" China asked.

"Sit for a while," I said, to bring to an end the song that was causing me such sorrow. "Tell me where you're from. Were you born in Amba Giorgis?" I patted the stool until she sat down and began to tell me her story.

"I was born in Chilga," she began, mentioning a place not too far from Gondar. "I was one of many children and we were very poor. You wouldn't know it to look at me now," she said proudly, pointing to the elaborate embroidery on her dress.

"I was like you, a village girl. I worked all day, just like you must have in your village—in the house, in the fields, fetching water, carrying around the babies that my mother had after me," she laughed and counted out her duties on her fingers.

"When I was about 10 years old, a man came to our village. He was a distant cousin of my mother. He stayed with us for a while and one day he caught me in the fields and raped me."

I gasped but said nothing. Her face looked tired suddenly and her shoulders slumped.

"My brothers were right nearby while this was happening to me," she said. "They were herding the sheep. I could hear the dogs barking and my brothers whistling and laughing. I could have called out to them and perhaps they would have made him stop. But he whispered to me that if I called out and my brothers came, he would have to kill them."

I sat completely still, watching the expressions pass over China's face. I felt as though what she was telling me was happening at that very moment and that I was there with her.

"When it was over, he said that he would hurt my brothers if I told anyone. But if I was a good girl, he would come back and bring me a beautiful doll."

"Did he come back?" I whispered.

"Yes, he did," she said.

"Did he do it to you again?"

"No, he did something much worse," China said sadly. "He told my parents that he'd found a job for me in Addis Ababa. He said that I would be working as a servant for a rich *faranj*. He promised that I would have a good life and be able to send money home."

China stopped talking and we looked at each other for a long moment.

"He sold me," she said quietly. "He sold me not to a rich foreigner but to a *tela beit* in Addis. I've been a prostitute ever since. But at least now I am free. Now I decide who I will sleep with and how much they will pay me."

"How did you get away from the *tela beit*?" I asked her.

"After a long time, I met a man there. He fell in love with me and bought me from the owner of the *tela beit*," she answered. "At first, he was careful to lock me in the house whenever he went out. But after a while he started to trust me. He believed that I loved him too." She shivered and fell silent for a moment, then went on. "One day he left without locking up the house. I knew where he kept his money. I stole from him and ran to the bus station."

"Why did you come here, to Amba Giorgis?" I asked after a moment of silence. "Why didn't you go home to your family?"

"At first, I was too ashamed to go home. And I was afraid that the man might come looking for me," she said. "But I'm not afraid anymore. It's been a long time since I left and my parents are no longer alive. So there isn't any reason to go back. I'm safe now and I'm happy," she said, and I was surprised to see her usual wide smile return so quickly to her face.

"Thank you for telling me your story," I said, hugging her warmly.

"Be careful, Wuditu," she warned. "You remind me of how I used to be—young, ignorant, only recently arrived from the village. You don't understand yet how things are in town. Don't let yourself be fooled. A pretty young girl like you, a virgin, is worth a lot of money, and there are men and women who would be happy to sell you. You can be taken before you even know what's happening. Promise me that you'll be careful!"

A few weeks later, government forces retook the town and the streets were again full of soldiers. Our afternoons were busy again, and one Saturday we were especially late in closing the *tela beit*. We were all tired and nervous from the constant gunfire. The soldiers shot off a round in the streets no matter what their mood—when they were drunk, when they were angry, when they were happy.

One of the soldiers had been hanging around China all night. She'd confessed to me that she was a bit afraid of him. On previous nights she'd tried to refuse him, but when he was drunk he could be violent and she'd admitted to me that it was often easier just to agree.

But that night, rather than threatening, he had begged and pleaded to go with her, offering to take her to a hotel and to buy her pretty clothes.

"Why are you being such a baby?" his friends shouted and made fun of his begging attitude.

"I'm no baby," he retorted angrily and grabbed China by the arm. "You're coming with me!" But no matter what he said or did, she kept refusing to go with him.

"You're always going off with anyone who asks you! So, why not with me? Is there something wrong with me?" he shouted.

"Of course there's nothing wrong with you." China tried to calm him. "I'm sick tonight. If I feel better I'll come with you tomorrow night. I promise."

The soldier wouldn't take no for an answer and soon his friends were arguing for him too. When China continued to refuse, the soldiers grabbed her and pulled her out of the house, describing what they would do to her when they got her alone.

Worried for my friend, I followed a ways behind them. I knew that I could do little to help besides following and hoping for a miracle. China was screaming and kicking out at the soldiers and I watched, terrified, when one of them pulled out his revolver and fired at her! The bullet whizzed past her ear and she fell to the ground.

I was about to run to her when Almaz came up behind me. Cursing fiercely, she dragged me back into the *tela beit* and slammed the door shut.

"Almaz, he may have killed her! We have to go out there!" I cried, struggling with her. But she glared at me and continued to hold the door closed. There wasn't a sound from outside the house, and when I made as though to try to open the door again, Almaz warned, "Don't you dare go out there! If you do, I won't let you back inside!"

I prayed for China all through the night, but she never came back. I was frightened for her but also for myself. *What a stupid girl you are for thinking you could be safe here!* I thought. *You thought you could live here and have a different life from that of the other girls. But you were wrong, very wrong!*

In the morning, after I had returned with our water, there was a knock on the door. It was the same soldier, and I watched as he dragged a barely conscious China into the living room. He dumped her onto the floor like a sack of *tef* and looked meaningfully in my direction.

"You're next," he said and then left.

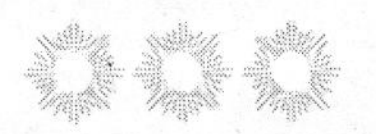

I could think of nothing but the soldier's threat, while Almaz and I tried our best to help China. Her wounds improved. But she was lost in herself and although she ate and drank, she had no will to speak or move around.

"If she doesn't get back to work soon, I won't be able to let her stay," Almaz said. "I can't afford to keep a girl without money."

Almaz gave China a week to recover and then told her to leave. I cried as I walked to the water pumps the next morning and prayed that the shock of being out on the streets would be enough to revive her. But in the evening, I found her just where I'd left her, sitting silently by Almaz's door, and that night I led her to the church and sat her down inside the fenced courtyard. At least there she'd be protected from the hyenas that roamed the streets at night.

China stayed there, in the open courtyard, for several days and those who took pity on her brought her food and water. Then one day she was gone and although I looked for her for weeks, I never learned what happened to her.

Chapter 15

Amba Giorgis, 1990

Wuditu, 14

For days I'd had a feeling of horror for what I knew was going to happen. But what choice did I have, except to kill myself? As terrible as my situation was, I didn't want to die. I prayed that I wouldn't suffer as badly as China.

When the soldier came, he was alone, without his friends, and I was grateful for that. "I'm taking you to a hotel," he said proudly. "It's a very nice place—you'll like it."

He took my arm and led me to another part of town. He acted as though I'd chosen freely to come with him. I nodded as though going to a hotel was a good thing. I thought that if I was nice to him he might not hurt me very much. But I stayed silent and kept on walking.

He was drunk but not too drunk. I could smell the liquor on his breath. It wasn't *tela*; it was something stronger. His breath was sickening, and I prayed that I wouldn't throw up in his face.

I was shocked when he put his hand on my breast—

right there in the street! He didn't seem to care that there were people all around us, that they could see what he was doing. I kept walking alongside him and as he moved his arm I caught sight of the revolver on his hip.

I thought, When we get to the hotel I could pull out his gun and threaten him. I could even shoot him and run away. But even as I thought it, I knew that it would do no good. There was no way to escape what was going to happen.

I stood silently beside him as he paid for the room and then followed behind him—up the stairs and down a long corridor. The room was small, the bed was narrow, and the sheets were badly stained. There was a half-full pail of water on the floor and two tiny towels folded on top of a small table. An electric light bulb hung from the ceiling, but it was giving off very little light. I could only be grateful for that.

It was cold in the room and I shivered when the soldier pulled my *kemis* over my head. I was filled with shame—no man had ever seen my body before. He looked me over and smiled, showing broken, dirty teeth.

He was surprised that I was pure. It made him feel proud. "You're a good girl," he said, pleased. "I'll keep you with me forever. I'll never let you go." He kept trying to turn my head toward his face, but I wouldn't let him kiss me.

That first night, he hurt me. But it wasn't the pain that was so hard to bear. It was the thoughts that came as I lay with my head turned to the wall. I remembered my mother, and what she used to say to me about a woman's body. "Purity is the most important possession a woman will ever own," my mother would say. And then she'd explain, "A female child walks a very different path from that of a boy. In our early years, we're allowed to move freely about the village. But as we grow closer to womanhood and start to go to the *mergem gojo*, our men begin to watch over us, making sure that no shame is brought upon our families.

"On your wedding night, while the guests are feasting, you'll be taken behind a special curtain. There, our female relatives will check if you are pure. If you are not, we'll all be disgraced and you may even be forced into leaving the village. That's why you must never let anyone take this precious thing away from you. Your husband is the only one who can do that."

So now I lay on the bed while the soldier slept. I wasn't alone, but I had no one to share my thoughts—that I was no longer pure, that now there would be no husband, there would be no children. My parents would never forgive me. But I wondered, What about God—would he forgive me? Was he watching? If he was watching, why hadn't he saved me?

I barely slept. Toward morning the soldier woke up. And when he took me for the second time, I cried.

The soldier continued to come for me night after night. As the days passed, I felt weighted down with shame at what I was doing. I moved around town on heavy, aching legs, my eyes cast downward. I was sure that everyone in Amba Giorgis knew what I had become.

After the first few weeks, when he sensed that I was not going to love him, the soldier began to complain and treat me roughly. "Don't I give you respect?" he asked. "I take you to a hotel so you won't be embarrassed to lie with me in the *tela beit*. I spend all my money on you and yet you remain cold."

I knew that if I wanted him to be gentler I had to try to please him. But time passed and I never did learn to pretend. And he never forgave me. No matter what I did, the nights always seemed to end with blows. Sometimes he'd bite me, like an animal. I started to be afraid that I might end up like China.

One night the soldier threatened that he'd give me to his friends. "Let them try to make you happy—I see that I can't," he shouted angrily.

I flung myself flat on the floor in front of him and begged. "I'll do anything you want. But please don't make me be with your friends," I moaned. "I'll kill myself before I let you do that!"

"Don't be stupid! I didn't mean it." He mumbled something I couldn't hear, turned his back to me, and went to sleep.

All through the next day, I prayed, "God, don't let this happen. I wanted only to earn an honest living and to find my family. And look what I've become! Please, show mercy—don't let him do this to me!"

That night the soldier didn't come for me. After several nights had passed with no sign of him, I asked Almaz, "Do you know what happened to him?"

"Why? Are you worried about him?" she sneered. "I'm not—he never did pay me very much. I think you'd better look for a richer customer."

"No, I was just wondering," I mumbled.

I never saw the soldier again. A few days later, I heard that he'd been sent to the front and that he was killed in a battle with the rebels. I was relieved and grateful. It was as though God had intervened to punish this man who had abused me.

But my relief didn't last long. My body had been changing over the last few weeks. My breasts were sore and my stomach was beginning to bulge, although, as usual, I had been eating very little. At first, I told myself that I must have some kind of stomach ailment. But eventually I had to accept that the soldier had made me pregnant.

I was overcome with despair. I looked down at my body with terror. How did I not see it before? Soon it would be obvious to anyone who looked at me. I'd have to hide my growing stomach from Almaz! If she saw that I was pregnant, she'd throw me out into the street. Then I'd have to go back to carrying water and sleeping wherever I could.

For just a minute, I thought, This baby is innocent! It doesn't deserve to die! I tried to imagine what my life would be like if I had to carry water all day and take care of a baby as well. Impossible! There was no way I could do that. As it was, I was barely eating enough to keep myself alive. That thought was swallowed up by a rush of others. What do I do now? How can I get rid of it? Who can I ask?

Over the next few days, I loitered in the market and at the water pumps. Who to ask? If I picked the wrong person, they might tell Almaz. Finally, I went back to the small hotel where the soldier and I had spent our nights. The owner was a man called Berreh. On occasion, we'd stopped to chat with him before going upstairs. He'd always treated us in a friendly manner. I was sure that I wasn't the first woman in his establishment to have this problem.

"It's been a while—how are you, Wuditu?" Berreh smiled widely as I entered the hotel. It had taken a lot of courage on my part to go back there. But I was desperate. Berreh looked at my expression and immediately took my arm, drawing me into his small office.

"What's wrong?" he asked kindly. I told him my problem, asking quietly, "Do you know how I can take care of it?"

There were several ways to deal with an unwanted pregnancy, he said, but they all cost money. He looked at me inquiringly and when I said that I had none, he asked if I wanted to work in the hotel, in which case he would lend me the money and I could repay him later.

I thanked him for his offer. It was very kind of him. I sat for a few minutes, thinking it over, and we sipped our coffee in friendly silence. I was grateful for his patience, but I knew that I couldn't consider his offer.

I was no longer pure. My time with the soldier had turned me into a prostitute. But agreeing to his offer would mean accepting prostitution as my fate. I thanked him politely and got up to go, with no other ideas about how I could get rid of the baby.

"I've heard..." Berreh started to say and then stopped, looking at me worriedly.

"Yes?" I said, with a glimmer of hope.

It was then that he told me there were things women could drink that might cause a pregnancy to end. "But it can be dangerous," he warned. "Women have died trying to kill their babies."

My hands were shaking when I stood over the fire that night. Almaz was asleep and there was no time to lose in preparing Berreh's recipe. I put large chunks of soap in a pot of boiling water. I pounded and then blended in the heads of matches and stirred it all together.

I wept bitterly as I worked. The smell was strong and I was afraid. What if I couldn't keep it all down? I had no idea what this brew would do to me. Frantically, I thought, What if it kills me as well as the baby? Who in my family would even know that I was dead? And even if they learned of my death, how would they know where to look for my body?

I moaned at the thought of lying in an unknown grave. Lewteh's face came to me and I thought, No matter what happens I want to live to see my sister again!

I forced myself to swallow it all in one gulp. I gagged and gagged, but I got the mixture down and kept it down. Still gagging, I rinsed out the pot so that Almaz wouldn't find out what I'd done. I was shaking badly and my heart was pounding while I gathered some folded rags, for I knew that if the potion worked, there would be bleeding.

I lay down and waited. Not too long after that, I started to have terrible cramps in my stomach and back. I was shocked by how strong the pains were and as they went on and on, I prayed that I hadn't done too much damage to myself as well as the baby. As the hours passed and the cramping worsened I began to pray that I wouldn't die.

I don't know how I had the strength to bear the pain.

At one point, I thought that I really would die, or at least lose consciousness. I worried about what Almaz would say if the rags gave out and I bled onto her pallet. Just when I thought that the night would never end, I felt the strongest cramp of all and I felt sure that the baby was gone.

I dragged myself to the back yard and buried the bloody pile of rags. I washed myself with the last of my strength and then I fell into a light and restless sleep. I wasn't sure where I was. Was I back in the village? In my delirium, I imagined that I must be in the *mergem gojo*. I imagined that the blood flowing out of my body was my own and not that of the baby that I'd killed.

Then I began to have a wonderful dream. I dreamed that it was my first time in the menstrual hut. I'd watched the other girls in the village and so I knew what was expected of me—to spend the next seven days and nights in the menstrual hut. Then, after the seventh day, I'd leave the hut and go down to the river to wash myself and my clothes, and to pray. Only at nightfall would I be pure. Then I could go back into our house.

In my dream, I wasn't afraid. What was there to be afraid of? From what I'd seen, the time spent in the *mergem gojo* was pleasant. Women passed the days gossiping, weaving baskets, and spinning cotton. Our female relatives brought us food and left it just outside the ring of stones that marked the area of ground that was impure.

But that first time, as it began to get dark, I realized that I would be the only female sleeping in the *mergem gojo* that night. I didn't want to be alone there in the dark, but I knew that I mustn't go back to my mother's house because the blood made me impure. Eventually, I crept out of the ring of stones and ran home. I leaned my body toward the doorway and cried out, "Enutie!"

"What is it, child?" my mother answered sleepily.

"I'm afraid to sleep alone, Enutie. What shall I do?" I wailed.

My mother and I couldn't touch each other, but that night we slept close together on the ground near our house. And the next day she sent my sister to keep me company. Lewteh sat outside the ring of stones until she saw another woman coming toward us and knew that I wouldn't be alone.

Chapter 16

Amba Giorgis, 1990

Wuditu, 14

"So, you killed your baby!" Almaz said when she found me the next morning. She sounded pleased and her next words confirmed it. "Good. I'm glad you decided not to keep it. How would you have been able to work if you had?"

I could barely keep my face set in a polite expression, for I knew that she meant, how would I be able to work for her?

"But next time, come to me before you do anything stupid," she said. "There are better ways to get rid of someone's bastard!"

Almaz had known all along that I was pregnant! I wondered how she had figured it out. She was a cold and businesslike woman, and I'd never expected any help from her, especially after she had turned China out into the street. But that morning, when I was too weak to get up, she surprised me by letting me rest that day and by taking away my soiled *kemis* for washing.

Soon after, I began to dream almost every night about

my life in Dibebehar. In my dreams, I'd have long talks with my mother and my sisters. "I've been with a man," I'd tell them. "He made me pregnant, but I couldn't keep it. So I killed my baby." In my dreams they understood and they weren't angry.

The dreams gave me comfort. One night, Lewteh called out to me and when I woke up, I remembered what it was she was trying to say—"Don't give up, Wuditu! Be strong!" I wondered, Could it really have been Lewteh, speaking to me so clearly in my dream? For the rest of that day, I felt her walking beside me, whispering in my ear.

I tried to keep my hopes high. I told myself that by now Lewteh might be in Yerusalem. If so, she would've told my father that I went to Amba Giorgis. Even if neither he nor Dawid could come for me, surely they would send someone. They wouldn't just leave me here to die!

Although in my dreams my family understood what I was going through, I knew that if I ever saw them again, I'd have to lie to them. And I'd have to live with those lies for the rest of my life. But getting to Yerusalem seemed a long way off and meanwhile I had to survive.

Ever since the soldier had stopped coming for me, Almaz had been saying that she was going to find me another customer. She kept asking, "Why are you working so hard when you could find another admirer and have an easy life?"

And I'd answer, "And if I did, who would do all the work around here?"

"Oh, that's no problem," she'd say. "I can always find another servant. All those stupid girls who come to town thinking they'll have a good life—they soon learn that it's better to work as a servant than to sleep in the street."

I didn't have to be reminded that there were girls, like China, who'd been captured and sold as slaves. No, Almaz would have no trouble replacing me if I chose to work as a prostitute. And she'd earn a fee from each of my customers. "My decision is final," I told her firmly.

"All right, if that's what you want," she said grudgingly. "Go ahead—if you want to kill yourself working as a servant, it's not my business."

But she never gave up. One day she said, "I have a better idea. Why don't you go to work as a servant for Elias, the teacher? He's offering a lot of money," she coaxed, speaking of a well-dressed customer who often came to the *tela beit*.

"I don't want to work for a man!" I protested. I knew very well that she'd be paid a fee for arranging this too.

"Let me speak to him and see what he says," Almaz answered.

Later that evening, she tried to reassure me. "You don't have to worry," she said. "I've spoken to Elias about you and he understands your conditions. He's not alone in the house. He lives with a young student boarder. He's looking for someone to do the cooking and the housework for the two of them."

When she saw that I wasn't going to agree, she looked at me sharply. "Don't be so stubborn! I'm telling you, the teacher is a very respectable man. Besides, he's responsible for young people. A man like that wouldn't do you any harm," she said.

I agreed to work at the teacher's house as long as I could continue to spend my nights on the back porch of the *tela beit*. Almaz promised to charge me less than her usual fee and I thought, This way, it'll take me less time to save the money I need.

The very next day I started working there. And just as Almaz said, Elias was very agreeable and so was the student, his nephew. It was easy to see that the two were related. They were both unusually tall and towered over me, although I am bigger than most girls. Elias walked with a stoop, as though apologizing for his height, but the nephew seemed to take pride in it. In time I came to believe that it wasn't arrogance but distraction that made him move about with his nose in the air.

Because the two were away for most of the day, I could set my own pace. After a few days, I began to relax a bit and to add up in my head the number of months I'd have to work to buy a bus ticket. I thought that a year was all that it would take. As the days passed, I'd find myself singing to myself as I worked. It was good to have hope again.

That first week, Elias bought me some new clothes because mine were old and much-mended. At first I protested when he brought them to me. "I can't afford new clothes," I said, handing them back to him and bowing respectfully.

"Oh, you don't need to pay me back," he assured me. "After all, you're a servant in my house and I have to keep up appearances. I can't have you working in rags," he explained.

Despite my discomfort at accepting clothes from someone who wasn't a relative, it was wonderful to have new things. And at the end of the first month, he paid me promptly for my services. He even added a few extra centimes.

"You've given me too much money," I said, handing the difference back to him.

"You should get some creams for your skin and hair," he said, waving the extra money at me. I accepted the money, realizing that I must look decent in the house of such a learned man.

Weeks went by and I was given a second month's wages. Again, Elias gave me money to buy myself a few luxuries and again, after protesting, I accepted the money. Soon, my hair was shining and my hands were soft from the creams that I had bought. I felt bad about spending the money on luxuries when I was saving for a bus ticket. But, after all, that was why my employer had given me the money—to improve my appearance.

Every time I went to fetch water I'd pass the mud kiosk and smile at the girl who wrote letters. Sometimes she'd wave back at me. I felt that we had become friendly. I kept thinking about asking her to write to my uncle Yonah in Gojjam, but I didn't have his address.

I'd been worrying about that—without an address, what would I write on the envelope? But recently I'd been thinking. I realized that I'd been to their home many years ago. I remembered how to get to their house and I could describe the way on the envelope. Even without an address, the letter might still get to them.

One day there were no customers at the kiosk and I stopped to speak to the girl.

"*Tenastelign*, good day," I began. My heart was beating loudly. She smiled and wished me a good day in return.

"Can you write a letter for me?" I asked.

"Of course," she answered.

"How much would it cost?" I asked.

She named a price, explaining that it included everything—the paper, the envelope, the stamp, and her work. I calculated that, God willing, I would have that much very soon.

"I don't have the exact address," I said, explaining that I wanted her to put the description of how to get to the family's house on the envelope.

"Oh, no, you can't do that!" she said, looking at me with a pitying expression.

"I can't? Why?" I asked. I felt that this conversation shamed me, although I didn't know why.

"It doesn't work like that," she answered. "You have to have a proper address on the envelope. The letter would never be delivered. You'd only be wasting your money."

I thanked the girl and walked off. I didn't want her to see how upset I was by our conversation. I'd been so excited to think that I might finally make contact with someone in my family. But I couldn't give up. There had to be a way.

I decided to ask Elias. He was an educated man, and perhaps he could help me figure this out. The next time he handed me my wages, I told him that I had an uncle in Gojjam and that I was saving up to join him there one day. In the meantime, I said, I wanted to write him a letter. I explained the problem and he confirmed that without an address, the letter most likely would never reach the family.

"Why don't you send it anyway, with the description? It doesn't cost that much to send a letter," Elias said. While I was thinking about it, he added, "Look. Why don't I pay for the letter?"

Elias's offer embarrassed me and made me a bit wary. What if I never heard back from my uncle? What would Elias expect from me in return for this gift?

When he saw me hesitating, he shoved the money into my hand, saying, "Here. I think you should send the letter. If he receives it, you can pay me back. If he doesn't get the letter, I have an idea—why don't you save for a bus ticket to Gojjam?" he suggested. "Once you're there, you can find him yourself."

I was delighted with this suggestion and I thanked him profusely for his help. The more I thought about it, the more I realized that this might be just the chance I needed to escape from this town and to find my way back to my people. In all the time since I'd left Lewteh, I'd heard nothing about any *faranj* messengers and I'd long ago given up looking for them. This way, I wouldn't be waiting for a chance encounter. I'd be relying on my own resources.

Elias was pleased and patted me affectionately on the back. Then he added, "If you want to save to go to Gojjam, it seems a shame for you to spend your wages on lodging at the *tela beit*. Why don't you stay here? There's plenty of room," he added with an encouraging smile.

I was a bit overwhelmed. What a good man! And how much money I would save by going to Gojjam, rather than Addis!

But then, I'm ashamed to admit, I started to worry. Why would he do such a thing? Was it really because he wanted to help me that he offered to let me sleep in his house for free?

But he pointed out that we weren't alone in the house

and that the living area had an adequate couch, which would be much more comfortable than my pallet in the back porch of the *tela beit*. Finally, I decided that I had much more chance of being harmed in the *tela beit* than in the teacher's house and agreed to try his suggestion for a few days.

"What're you afraid of?" Almaz laughed when I discussed the matter with her. "I've told you, he is a decent man. Don't you believe me?"

That night I slept with one eye on the teacher's room. But he never disturbed me. He seemed to be developing a fatherly affection for me and after a while I began to relax and to enjoy the comfort and privacy.

Over the summer holidays, Elias's nephew went back to his parents' village. At first, I worried about being alone in the house with Elias, but as the days passed I began to relax again, knowing that in only a few months I would be able to go to Gojjam. Soon my troubles would be over!

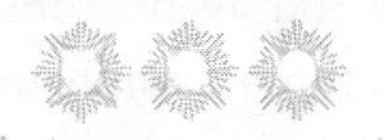

When the vacation ended, Elias's nephew returned to Amba Giorgis. That first afternoon he went out—to see his schoolmates, I thought. I was half asleep on my couch when he returned. When he passed by me on the way to his room, I was surprised to smell liquor on his breath. This was the first time that he had come home after drinking and at first I thought to tease him. But I quickly changed my mind, telling myself that although I took care of his things like a mother, it wasn't my place to tell him how to behave.

Bam! I woke up with a start a few minutes later but relaxed again when I realized that Elias's nephew had knocked something over in his room. "The kid is drunk," I laughed to myself and relaxed into my comfortable bed.

Soon after that, he entered the living room on shaky legs and I saw that he was indeed very drunk. He must have brought a bottle with him from home. I watched in growing fear as he made his way slowly and deliberately toward the couch.

"Get up!" he hissed at me in a voice I'd never heard before. His face was grim, and while I was still trying to decide what to do, he grabbed me by the arm and pulled me off the couch.

"You're sleeping with me tonight!" he whispered, pulling me across the living room and into his room.

"No, I am not!" I shouted back at him. "Let me go! You're drunk!"

"Shut up," he said, still whispering, and pushed me down onto his bed. I landed face first and twisted around frantically, trying to roll away from him. I screamed as loudly as I could and fought wildly until I heard footsteps thudding toward us.

"What's the matter with you?" Elias screamed, pulling his nephew off the bed. He smacked him hard on the cheek and pushed him down onto the floor.

Elias pulled me to my feet and continued pulling me, muttering, until I was back on the couch, curled up and shivering.

"I'm so sorry," he said, covering me with my *netela* and patting it awkwardly around me. I could see that he was terribly upset. "I feel responsible," he said sadly. "I can't believe what he tried to do! Are you all right? How badly did he hurt you?"

"I'm fine," I sobbed. "Thank God you heard my screams."

That night, all I could think of was that I would have to leave this house that had seemed so safe. And worse, my plan to save money to go to Gojjam would have to wait. I'd have to go out into the streets again and try to make my living as I had before. Who knows how long it would take before I had enough for a bus ticket.

Hours later, when Elias saw that I meant to go, he didn't look surprised. "Where will you go?" he asked sadly.

I felt bad for him. He had been so good to me and he clearly didn't want me to go. He even seemed worried about me. It had been a long time since someone had cared what would happen to me.

"I'll go back to Almaz," I said, shrugging as though it didn't matter and wanting to make my leaving easier for him. I left Elias's house, carrying a small amount of money and my few possessions in a scarf that he had bought for me in happier days. I knocked on the door of the *tela beit* with a terrible sense of defeat.

"You are a fool," Almaz sneered before I could say a word of explanation. "You could have had a good life with him."

Chapter 17

Amba Giorgis, 1990

Wuditu, 14

In the morning I said good-bye to Almaz and left the *tela beit* for what I hoped would be the last time. Almaz must have guessed what I was thinking because she assured me, "You can come back any time."

I went back to carrying water for people in the town. But I didn't have any idea what I would do when night fell. So all day I trudged back and forth along the dusty paths, carrying water and thinking about where I would sleep. Some of my former customers remembered me and asked where I had been.

"I went to a wedding," I answered and made up a story about a cousin in a distant village. I was shocked at how easily the lies came to me now. When it got dark I decided that I would try to sleep outside for one night, in the shadow of a bridge I'd often passed. I knew it wasn't the safest place to be, but I didn't really have a choice.

The roads were always lined with the white-wrapped,

huddled forms of people who had no money to pay for a bed. But that night, as I'd hoped, there was no one else sleeping under the bridge. So I cleared a patch of ground and lay down. I tried to go to sleep, but I was frightened. It was cold outside and I shivered in my thin *netela*.

I prayed. "Amlak Israel, God of Israel, keep me safe out here in this dark place. Protect me until morning comes!"

But as I lay there, unable to sleep for the cold and my fear, I started to feel angry at how my life was unfolding and I began to argue with him. "How can this be what you planned for me? What kind of a God would abandon me this way? Would a merciful God let me sleep out in the open, where I might be eaten by a pack of hyenas?"

Finally, I fell asleep. During the night, people passed quite close by me in the dark, talking in loud voices. In my dreams they turned into thieves, about to rob me of the few birr I'd managed to save. Once during the night, I dreamed that something was breathing close to my ear, something low, like a dog.

I woke up with a terrible cry! "Aiiee!! *Minden now*, what is it?!" I shrieked and threw my arms around wildly. But there was nothing there, nothing but shadows on the ground and the bridge above me.

I tried to go back to sleep. I thought about my friend China and remembered what had happened to her when she could no longer work. In the last few weeks, sores had appeared all over my arms and my legs. They were itchy, open, and leaking. Was this the beginning of some strange disease? I was tired all the time now, and sometimes, especially toward the end of the day, my legs felt like they might collapse under me. What would happen to me if I got sick and could no longer work?

My body had never felt the same since the abortion. My monthly bleeding never came back, as though it were saying, You were wicked and now even your body is punishing you. You'll never bleed again. You'll never have a child.

As I lay there, I held my head in my hands, pleading to be rid of these terrible thoughts. "Leave me alone! Let me sleep. Please, God—let me sleep!"

Toward morning, I tried to stand but fell back in pain. I was aching all over from my night on the cold, hard ground and my legs were trembling and weak. For just a minute I thought, Maybe it would have been a good thing if I had been eaten during the night.

As quick as the thought came, it vanished, replaced by Lewteh's voice, shouting as she had in my dream: "Be strong, Wuditu!" Like a *ketab*, a talisman, hanging around my neck, her voice came. And suddenly I wanted so much to survive and to see my sister again!

My legs found their strength and I stood up and began walking. I told myself that my plan to get to Gojjam was a good one. I just needed to earn a bit more money. All I had to do was to find somewhere where I could be safe until then. I'm coming to you, Lewteh, I thought and promised my sister that I'd never sleep outside again.

All through the next day, I went back and forth along the narrow alleys of Amba Giorgis. I didn't carry water or do any other work. I didn't eat and I didn't beg for food. I just kept asking everyone I met if they needed a servant. I knew that if I didn't manage to find work in the next few days, I might be too weak from hunger to go back to carrying water. But I sensed that I was already too weak to keep on the way I had been working and I was becoming desperate.

Maybe it was that desperation in my voice or perhaps God heard my prayers, for early on the first day of my search, one of my customers suggested, "Why don't you go talk to the *meloxie*? I've heard that her granddaughter is looking for help."

I prayed that this was the chance I'd been searching for. I followed the woman's directions to a small stone house a few streets away. By the doorway was a battered tin cup, turned upside down on a pole. This was the sign of a place where alcohol was served—in this case not *tela* but *arakie*, a beer that took much longer to brew.

A fat old woman was sitting near the doorway, her backside spilling out over a small, three-legged stool. She looked up as I came near, and I saw that she had beautiful light green eyes and a pleasant expression on her plump face. A wooden cross lay on her breast, and she held a rosary in her hands and murmured softly to herself.

Having lived among the townspeople for a while, I knew that a *meloxie* was a Christian who'd had a normal life but now lived like a nun, renouncing worldly things and making a vow to the church to spend the rest of her life praying. I looked at the woman's kindly expression and thought, How I would like to work for a person like that, someone who does nothing but pray!

"Good day, how are you?" I asked, bowing low and speaking in a respectful tone.

"I am well, God be thanked," she answered and waited for me to speak.

"I'm an orphan and I've left my village. I'm looking for work as a servant," I began. I felt that all my future depended on this woman's goodwill. What could I say or do to make her decide in my favor?

"Where are you from?" she asked.

"I'm from Semien," I answered, naming the mountainous region where I'd grown up.

"I, too, am from Semien," she smiled and we spoke of our villages, which were only a few days' walk from each other.

"Are you a good Christian girl?" she asked, searching my face.

"Of course," I answered, bowing deeply again. For the first time in my life, I made the sign of the cross. I prayed that God would forgive me. The gesture seemed to reassure her.

"My granddaughter is looking for someone to help her in the *arakie beit*," she answered, looking me over. "The work is hard. I see that you are very tall. Are you also strong?"

"Oh, yes, I am very strong!" I answered. "If your granddaughter will give me a chance, I'll work very hard for her."

"Wait here a minute," she said, lifting herself up with great difficulty and making her way into the house. She returned a moment later with a woman in her 20s. "This is my granddaughter, Yelemwork," she said.

The young woman was very beautiful—as beautiful as her name, which means "a golden world." She had the same bright green eyes as the *meloxie* and the kind of wavy hair that is very rare and much prized. But her face, despite its beauty, wasn't open and inviting like her grandmother's, and as she questioned me in the street her manner was very abrupt.

"I will pay you five birr a month," she said and motioned me into the house.

That night I slept on a pallet in Yelemwork's living room. I shared the room with the family cow—which they called "the great one." I was afraid that it might kick me in the head. It didn't, but it peed on the floor right beside me, and sometime during the night I dreamed that I was in my father's village and that it was Lewteh, not "the great one," who'd wet our bed.

It was still dark when Yelemwork poked me, hissing, "Did you come here to work or to dream? Get up and go bring water, you lazy girl!"

Part Four

The Arakie Beit

Chapter 18

Amba Giorgis

Wuditu, 14

Yelemwork's house was small, square, and made of stone. In it, there were only my mistress, her little son and daughter, the *meloxie*, and now me. The inner walls of the whole house were plastered with mud, to make it warmer in the winter months. I spent most of my time in the back porch, cooking and cleaning and brewing the *arakie* that my mistress served to customers in her living room.

The living room walls were decorated with photographs cut out of magazines. My favorite was the one of a beautiful young girl in a gray dress. Her hair was arranged in many small braids, and each one had been carefully beaded. When I looked at it, it reminded me of how Lewteh and I used to braid each other's hair. Sometimes I'd tell myself that it was Lewteh in the picture. She looked a little like my sister, and sometimes I'd smile at her when I passed by. Lewteh had always been the keeper of my secrets, and it comforted me to pretend that I could still confide in her.

Above the picture was written, "Ethiopia: 13 Months of Sunshine." I'd seen it before—it was from the tourist office and it used to hang in our classroom in Dibebehar. The teacher had explained to us that while in Ethiopia there are 13 months in the year, many other countries have only 12 months because they use a calendar that's different from ours.

I knew from the very first day that Yelemwork wasn't going to be a kind mistress. But that didn't seem so terrible after what I'd already suffered. Even though she sold *arakie* in her living room, I didn't think Yelemwork would take men into her bed at night. After all, there was a holy woman living in the house and Yelemwork herself had a young daughter. Would she let men rent mats in her living room? It didn't seem likely, so I was pleased. I'd found a safe place to stay.

So even though the weather was cold and damp, I sang to myself as I walked to the water pumps early that first morning. The pumps were about a half-hour's walk from Yelemwork's house and were built on natural springs. After filling up your jugs, it was sometimes necessary to wait a long time before the water level rose again, especially during the dry season. So I wasn't surprised when Yelemwork woke me up well before daylight. If you wanted to make two or three trips for water and still get your morning chores finished, you had to get there early.

As I made my way back and forth through town over the next few weeks, I spoke to no one. I was used to keeping to myself. At most, I nodded to people whom I started to recognize. I never stayed to chat. I was always afraid that I might accidentally do or say something to make people realize that I was Beta Israel.

I was right to be afraid. I'd seen that people in Amba Giorgis were just as superstitious as the villagers in Dibebehar, and every time I heard someone say the word *falasha* my heart would pound. On my very first day, I came across Helen, the woman who lived in the house next door. She and Yelemwork often had coffee in each other's houses, and on that day, Helen was telling Yelemwork and the *meloxie* a story. She'd been north to her sister's village and a young pregnant woman there had gotten very sick.

"She didn't have a fever or any other signs of illness," she said. "But time had passed and she still didn't get any better. Her husband, who is a wealthy man, brought her a real nurse, all the way from town. The nurse examined her and said, 'This woman is completely healthy. There's nothing wrong with her. But for some unknown reason, she seems to be dying!'"

Helen paused to take a sip of coffee while we all waited to hear what she would say next.

"The village elders held a council," she continued. "They investigated the matter and quickly came to the conclusion that it was a *falasha* from the other side of the village who had put a spell on the woman!"

"Oh, my God, that's terrible!" Yelemwork murmured. The *meloxie* fingered her cross and said a prayer for the unknown woman. I stood, paralyzed, with a jug of water suspended in the air. Yelemwork nudged me, annoyed, and I poured more water into the coffee pot. Act normally, I told myself. Don't give yourself away.

"What happened to that poor young woman?" the *meloxie* asked anxiously.

"Hah! The *falasha* confessed!" Helen said triumphantly. "We only had to shake him up a little and right away he told us everything. Of course, we forced him to remove the curse he'd put on the woman. And the proof of his guilt could be seen in the fact that she right away got up and started cooking!"

"But what about this *falasha*, what did they do to him?" Yelemwork asked.

"We banished him from the village, of course—him and his whole family!" Helen answered. "After all, he could have done the same thing to someone else."

I kept my face blank and left as soon as I was no longer needed. It wouldn't do to show my fear. I didn't need any further reminder that my life would be in danger if they found out that I was a Jew. All I could do was keep to myself and pray that I could save enough money to leave this house.

Yelemwork had promised me five birr a month. But at the end of the first month she didn't pay me. Every day I waited for her to give me my wages and every day nothing happened. I was afraid to say anything but eventually I was more afraid not to. When two more months went by I dared to ask, "Mistress, when will I receive my wages?"

"Wages," Yelemwork sniffed. "You came to me in rags and I had to give you my own clothes. Did you think I'd give you my things for nothing? Certainly not! You'll have to pay me back by working it off."

I was very angry. I hadn't come to her in rags, but after a while, working as hard as I did, my clothes had begun to wear thin. The ones she gave me to replace them were just as old and mended and in any case, she had planned to give them away to the church. Why should I have to pay for them?

But I was afraid to say anything that might make Yelemwork look at me too carefully. I'd been feeling ill. My legs sometimes shook with tiredness and the ugly sores on my body itched unbearably. I was scared that if she saw how weak I was getting, she might throw me out.

It didn't help that I was always hungry. By the time I came back from carrying water, the family had usually finished their morning meal. "Take something to eat from what's left over," Yelemwork would say, waving a hand toward the back porch as I staggered into the house with my heavy jugs.

Most of the time, there was only a small piece of *injera* bread, sometimes with a bit of *wot*, a sauce made of vegetables and lentils or beans. If there was time, I'd take a spoonful of sourdough batter and start to fry some more bread for myself. But Yelemwork often had me starting on some other task before I'd had a chance to eat.

I could have said something to the *meloxie* about my wages, but I was afraid to take a chance. Although she was the head of the household and greatly revered for her religious beliefs, it was actually Yelemwork who was in charge and her anger frightened me. Once, I did say something to the *meloxie* about being hungry. She answered, "That's how it is, child. *Tigist*, patience, you must learn to be patient," and quoted a saying about patience that I had learned to hate—"slowly, slowly, the egg will walk on its own legs."

But from then on, she paid more attention to my comings and goings. When she saw that much of the day had already passed and I still hadn't eaten, she would put her hand on my shoulder and say, "Take a plate of food and come out into the sunshine with me, child. Let us chat a while about the place of our birth," or some other frivolous excuse.

This was an outrageous thing to do—to invite a servant to sit around and gossip with you! It was unheard of. But, fortunately for me, someone as holy as the *meloxie* could get away with that kind of behavior.

Yelemwork would grit her teeth and glare at me. But she didn't dare contradict her grandmother. It wouldn't take long before she'd have me up and running to complete some task. But at least I would have eaten.

The *meloxie*'s small interventions made my situation a little more bearable. Even so, I thought about leaving after several months had passed and I still hadn't been paid. But the thought of being out in the streets again was just too frightening. And, without money for bus fare, where would I go? After a while, I began to lose hope. The more I thought about it, the more I realized that without meaning for it to happen, I'd become Yelemwork's slave.

My days in the *arakie beit* were always the same—week after week, month after month. On Sundays, people rested and went to church. But my day would start as usual at the water pumps. After returning, I'd put a large basket on my head and hurry out to the fields where animal dung, which we used as fuel, was drying in the sun.

I didn't like this job. I hated the smell that lingered afterward, no matter how much I washed my hands. Some people in Amba Giorgis used wood for fuel, but now that so much of the forest had been cut down near the town it was too far to go to collect firewood. And to buy wood was expensive. "Why should we pay for it when this is just lying in the fields, free for the taking?" Yelemwork rightly insisted.

It was also, for me, dangerous work. The first time I went out to collect animal dung, I came across a group of young men who had taken their animals out to pasture. Bored by their work, they were delighted to see me coming their way and I had to run desperately back toward town to escape them.

Luckily, a group of children came by and I made sure to stay close to them. After that, I learned to delay going out as long as I could, until I saw others heading toward the fields.

Since it was Sunday and there was no school, sometimes Yelemwork's young son and daughter would come along with me. As we came back into the house, hot and tired and smelling of dung, the children would be given a warm welcome.

"Oh, you are such good children—look at how much you have brought! Why, your baskets are so full! You must be tired," Yelemwork would croon. She'd pet and kiss the children and rush them into the living room to wash their hands and faces before their afternoon meal.

I'd come to love Yelemwork's children and I never begrudged them their mother's affection. But there were times that I couldn't stop a knot of jealousy from curling inside my chest. There was no one to pet and feed me, and some days there wasn't even time for me to eat, with my mistress's sharp eyes always watching me.

On Mondays I took the grains to the mill for grinding. By the time I finished bringing water there was usually a long lineup at the mill. Once I'd handed the flour over, I either had to wait my turn or come back several times to check if it was ready to be taken away.

Back at the house, I'd sift the grains and prepare the batter for the family's *injera*. Fresh batter had to be left to ferment for several days so I had to make sure that there was enough of the old batter to last us until the new one was ready. I'd have felt happier about this part of my work if I'd been able to eat whenever I was hungry. As it was, it was just another task to keep me occupied.

On Mondays, I had another important job, one that earned the funds that kept the household running. That was to prepare the *arakie* for the customers. Brewing *arakie* was a tiresome job. It took nearly a week before it was ready and had to be kept on the fire and watched over at all times. In comparison, the *tela* I'd brewed for Almaz had taken only three days and it didn't need to be constantly tended to.

Every Saturday I went with Yelemwork to the town market. While she chatted with her neighbors and bargained over goods, I stood still, holding her purchases. Most of the time, I was ragged and filthy and so it wasn't a surprise that no one ever spoke to me. Standing there silently, like a beast that carried goods, I felt more than ever like what I had become—a slave.

As time went on, my hair became dull and lifeless and grew wild. I tried to keep it in tight braids, but much of the time I was too busy to think about what the wind and my hard work were doing to it.

Yelemwork, with her beautiful, shining waves, pretended not to notice. But one day she handed me a length of thin, black material to cover my head, saying with a sneer, "Can't you do something about that messy bush of yours?"

I tied it tightly around my head, furious, and thought, How many days will I have to work to pay you back for this ugly rag?

My body was now pocked by open sores and I was filthy most of the time. But for some reason, the condition of my hair bothered me almost more than anything else. Someday I'll be in Yerusalem, I'd promise myself. I'll have lots of money and I'll pay someone to wash and oil and arrange my hair. Lewteh's too, and all my sisters, and what a good time we'll have then!

Every once in a while, I considered dipping my hand into some of Yelemwork's jars of hair cream, but I was too frightened of being caught stealing. As for my sores, it amazed me that no one had said anything about them. One day, when I couldn't bear the itching any longer, I showed them to the *meloxie*.

"Don't worry, child, I'll tell you what to do," she said in her soft, musical voice. "You must gather the great one's pee and pour it over your sores—every morning and every night. Every day and every night," she repeated, "and soon—you'll see—they'll dry up and they won't bother you anymore."

Although I had little faith in the cow's urine as a cure, I tried it out of respect for the *meloxie*. I found to my surprise that the wounds did, in fact, dry up. They left terrible scars, but they didn't itch as they once had.

"How are your sores, child?" the *meloxie* inquired a few days later.

"Much better, thanks. See?" I answered, holding out my arms.

This was the only time in the years I lived there that anyone in that house ever asked about my health. I treasured that moment and served the *meloxie* even more devotedly from then on.

Chapter 19

Amba Giorgis, 1991

Wuditu, 15

Over the last year, I'd learned that the *meloxie* liked to start her day with a warm glass of *arakie*. So every morning when I came back from the water pumps, I'd heat up a glass for her and take it into her room. "Ooh, that's so good!" she'd say and smile sweetly at me. "It warms my old bones."

The *meloxie*'s smiles meant a lot to me. I was alone most of the time. Before, when I'd carried water, people had looked at me and talked with me. I'd felt real. But ever since I'd started to work for Yelemwork, people didn't look at me anymore or speak to me—except to tell me what to do. So I told myself, No matter how bitter my days are, at least they always start with a smile from the *meloxie*.

Every once in a while, she would put her hand on my head and say a prayer over me. I wanted to show my gratitude so sometimes I'd make the sign of the cross right along with her. I knew that it was wrong, but this small thing bound us together.

I believed that God would forgive me for betraying my faith. But one day I remembered a time in Sudan when Lewteh had spoken a few words from the Muslims' prayer. I was so angry with her for doing that! Now I worried that I was doing the same thing. Would I become something other than what I was taught to be?

There was only one other person who showed me some kindness during those lonely months—Berreh, the hotel owner who was a regular customer in the *arakie beit*.

When the rebel army first took Amba Giorgis, they looked for a man of goodwill, someone who could restore order while they continued to fight to liberate Ethiopia. Even though Berreh had fought with Mengistu, he had a lot of influence in town. So the rebels decided that, although he wasn't one of their own, he was just the kind of person they needed.

Berreh had 10 years of schooling so he was much more educated than most of the townspeople. He was well liked in Amba Giorgis for his generosity as well as his wisdom, and he was also a prosperous businessman. When I had worked carrying water, he had sometimes taken pity on me and let me sleep in his hotel without paying.

When I first realized that he was one of Yelemwork's customers, I was terrified that he would spread gossip about me. But even though he knew me before I came to the *arakie beit*, he never said a word to anyone about my time with the soldier and I came to believe that he never would.

The rebels had armed Berreh well—he had a pistol, a rifle, and a long, curved knife, and he always wore a thick leather belt packed with bullets that crossed his shoulders and continued down and around his waist. In spite of all this, I knew that Berreh was a peace-loving man, and while at first he had frightened me, I eventually came to ignore all the weapons he carried.

Berreh was different from most of the other soldiers I'd known. Like them, he loved to drink and gossip and joke with the other customers. But he could also be very courteous and open-minded. Perhaps it was because he owned a hotel, but he didn't seem to have any bad opinions about women like me who had worked as prostitutes. He treated us like everyone else, with the same polite attention.

Like most of the other soldiers, he was a heavy smoker. But in consideration for the *meloxie*, who hated the smell, he always stepped outside to smoke in the back porch where I worked. While he smoked we would talk and sometimes I'd find myself speaking much too freely. Once or twice I even spoke to him of my uncle in Gojjam and of my wanting to find a way to get there. I told him that my uncle was a teacher and that he was rich.

"You certainly won't have to work when you get there," he said. "Will you come back and see us after you have become a fancy lady?"

"Of course, every year," I answered haughtily, waving my spoon about and nearly knocking over the container of *arakie* that was steaming on the fire.

"Watch it, that's boiling hot!" he warned.

"I'd hate to start this brew all over again if it spilled." I laughed.

"What presents will you bring me when you come to

visit?" he asked with a smile.

"What would you like?" I responded.

"Ah, there are so many things I want," he answered thoughtfully.

"What kind of things?" I asked.

"If you ever get to Gojjam, bring me some books when you come to visit us," he said. "Your uncle can surely recommend some good ones."

I'd been expecting something totally different, something new and shiny, like a transistor radio. But I shouldn't have been surprised. Berreh had often spoken about how sorry he was that he hadn't been able to continue his education. He didn't seem bitter about it. He just spoke of it as a fact.

Berreh was the only one who ever talked to me like a person, not a slave. Perhaps it was because he knew me before I had become one. He even asked my opinion about a lot of things that were happening in town and he listened carefully whenever I spoke. I was so grateful for these few moments because I'd come to feel that the part of me that thought and spoke and listened was gone, replaced by a body that only walked and bent and carried.

Although I'd come to trust him in some ways, I had to keep reminding myself of what might happen if he discovered that I was a *falasha*. Sometimes I wondered if it would matter to him. He has such power, I sometimes thought. If I could only tell him who I am, what has happened to me, and how far I am from home, perhaps he would help me. But the risk was too grave and I never did tell.

In the beginning, I tried to have some conversation with Yelemwork. After I finished a task that was new to me, I would stop and ask, "Did I do that right? Was that what you wanted?"

I was hoping for a kind word or a bit of conversation. As a child, I'd been petted and treasured by my mother and at first I wanted some praise in return for my long hours of work. Yelemwork didn't seem to understand what I was asking for. She never beat me, but she was cold and demanding, and no matter how hard I worked, she was never satisfied.

The months went by and then one day I realized that I'd been there for more than two years. I was still working and I was still unpaid. I was much weaker than I had been when I first came to the *meloxie*. And I was sick but didn't realize it at first. I was much more resigned about my life, and I just wanted to get through the days, to drop down onto my pallet at night and sleep.

One night I felt among my bedclothes and found that the few birr I'd saved at the teacher's house was gone. It wasn't very much. But it was all I had. At the beginning, I'd thought of asking Yelemwork to hold it for me. But when she didn't pay me, I decided to keep it in my pallet. Now that it was gone, I was upset by the loss, but I had too little strength to do anything about it.

One day I woke up and realized that it was Timkat, the Christianos' Easter. That meant that it was also our Fasika—and I hadn't even realized it! Our holidays had come and gone and I'd had no way to celebrate them. I realized that for two years I hadn't marked the Sigd, the day we went up to the top of a mountain and prayed facing Yerusalem.

On that day the whole village fasted and prayed that

one day we would return to our homeland. I had missed this important day not once but twice, possibly even three times! I wasn't sure. The last one would have been months ago. But I thought that it would be better to mark the day late rather than not at all. So as I worked I fasted that whole day and prayed that I would find a way to go home to my family and to my people.

That evening I collapsed—right in the middle of Yelemwork's coffee cups! Fortunately, I didn't break any of her dishes or I would have had to pay for them. But this I only found out later, because at the time I was unconscious.

When I woke up, I found that my pallet had been moved from the living room to the back porch, so I wouldn't infect the children or the customers. I lay there for days or for weeks—I'm not sure for how long. My sores drove me mad. I burned with fever and my head ached.

I had no idea what illness this was. Time went on and I was not getting well. When I was awake I tried to believe that it would end one day and I would still be alive. I prayed whenever I was awake. I curled up as small as I could and whispered, "Amlak Israel, Amlak Israel!" There was nothing in the whole world but those two words, *Amlak Israel, Amlak Israel*, pounding in my head.

It seemed that it must have been the *meloxie* who answered my prayers—because after a time she sent a friend to come and give me injections. I don't know if that was what healed me but soon after that I began to sit up and after a while I could even move about for a few minutes at a time.

While I was sick, Berreh had come out often to smoke,

and I had memories of him bending down to feed me sips of water. In our language, the name Berreh means "a gate opens." As I lay burning with fever one night, I saw his face bending over me and I pleaded, "Amlak Israel—open a new doorway for me!"

I feared that in my fever I might have let my secret slip. But if I had, Berreh didn't mention it.

Chapter 20

Amba Giorgis, 1992

Wuditu, 16

It was only a few days after I got up from my sickbed when a young woman came to town and rented a place from Helen, the lady next door. I recognized her immediately. It was Hailu, my former schoolmate from Dibebehar!

I told myself that she might not recognize me. I was so much skinnier than I'd been then and I was dressed in rags. Most people passed me by without even looking at me.

Hailu said not a word to me. Instead, she went back into the house next door and shouted out in a loud voice, "What's that girl doing here in Amba Giorgis? I thought all the *falashas* left long ago—why didn't she go to Israel with the rest of her family?"

Nothing happened that first night. But the silence was terrifying. I was so scared I couldn't sleep. I wondered, Is it possible that Yelemwork didn't hear what the girl said? She was right there when it happened. If she heard the girl, why didn't she say something?

Then I thought, Even if she did hear, I can still deny that I'm a *falasha*. It's Hailu's word against mine. Whatever happened, I mustn't let them see that I was worried.

The next day I came back from the water pumps to find Yelemwork missing. She'd gone next door to Helen's for her morning coffee. "Good morning!" I sang out when I brought the *meloxie* her glass of *arakie*. She greeted me politely, but there was no smile for me that morning and no prayers for my good health.

I went about my work as though nothing unusual had happened, but my thoughts raced and my head ached with the waiting and the fear.

"Wuditu, get in here! We need some more water," Yelemwork called through Helen's doorway a few minutes later, and I bowed low as I entered the house next door. Usually, Yelemwork took great care to appear a decent mistress. She might treat me badly in her own house, but when she was at the neighbors' or in the market, her behavior was always correct.

But this time, she made no effort to conceal her contempt and as I moved toward Helen, she pushed me forward roughly, even though I was carrying boiling water. I righted myself and tried to act as though it hadn't happened.

Helen didn't seem at all surprised at this abrupt change of attitude. I could only assume that the two women had discussed Hailu's revelation. I was terrified, but I tried to hide my fear. I smiled widely as I poured the water into Helen's coffee pot. "Mistress, do you need anything else?" I inquired, bowing deeply.

Everyone in the room was silent, watching me, weighing

my response to Yelemwork's behavior. I waited, trying to pretend that I didn't see any change, that I didn't see their conspiratorial nods and meaningful looks.

When no answer came, I bowed again and left the house. In the back porch, I wiped my tears. I will not give myself away! I promised myself. They may try to trap me, but they'll have to do it without my help!

I went on with my chores, all the while trying desperately to appear as though everything was normal. Later in the day I overheard the *meloxie* say, "The girl's been living with us for more than two years and she's never lied to us in all that time. Why should we believe the word of someone we've just met? She could be wrong in thinking that our Wuditu is the girl she knew in Semien."

But the *meloxie*'s words hadn't convinced Yelemwork. Just before the customers were due to arrive, my mistress called me into the living room. "You've lied to us," she said angrily. "You said you were a Christian, just like us. But you're not a Christian. You are an evil *kayla*!" Yelemwork spat.

I gave her a look of surprise and turned to the *meloxie*, bowing low. "Have I offended you in some way?" I asked innocently.

Her face was troubled and she didn't answer me.

"When you first came to us, my grandmother asked if you were a good Christian girl and you said that you were. Now we've learned that you're a *falasha*!" Yelemwork spat at me again.

"Why would you think that I'm a *falasha*?" I inquired, as though puzzled.

"We have a witness—Hailu, your former schoolmate,

told us all about you. You're the daughter of a *falasha* potter. This girl knows you very well," she added. "You might as well tell us the truth. Tell me quickly why I shouldn't have you whipped and thrown to your cousins, the hyenas!"

"Listen to me," said one of her customers, who'd arrived early and overheard the conversation. "You've fed her and kept her for a long time. You should try to recover the money you've spent on her. If I'd been deceived like that, I'd make the girl work until she died of exhaustion," he said with a nasty look in my direction.

"If that's what you decide to do, you should first make sure that she doesn't run away," another customer said. "You can cut off one of her feet," he suggested, and I gasped and backed away as far as I could get. "See, she's already trying to get away!" he said, pointing a thick finger in my direction. "Yes, cut off one of her feet. She'll still be able to work for you, but she won't be able to run away so easily and her powers will be greatly reduced. A wounded *falasha* is much less powerful than a healthy one, you know," he said, and the others nodded, impressed with his logic.

"It's dangerous to have a *falasha* in your house, even a wounded one. Maybe it's better just to kill her," said a third customer, and he moved toward me with his arm raised over his head.

"But it's not true! I'm *not* a *falasha*," I shrieked and continued to back away while the group moved threateningly toward me.

"Stop that, all of you! This is my house and this girl is my servant!"

Everyone stood still, surprised to hear the *meloxie*

speak so sharply. "I'll decide what's to be done with her," she said firmly. "Meanwhile, except for that stranger's story we have no reason to believe that Wuditu is a *falasha*. In all the time she's been here, has she harmed any of us? No, she hasn't!"

"She's been very clever, hiding here. There's still time for her to do so." Yelemwork shuddered, making the sign of the cross.

"Come, everyone—come and have a drink," the *meloxie* interrupted Yelemwork, squeezing between the customers and holding me firmly by the arm. The crowd slowly backed away from me and headed toward the living room, while the *meloxie* spoke to her granddaughter in a soothing tone. "Yelemwork, you and I will talk about this later and then we'll decide what's to be done."

That afternoon, the *meloxie* had the last word. She led me to the back porch and pushed me down onto my pallet. "Stay here, girl!" she hissed. "And make sure you keep well away from everyone for the rest of the evening."

Although she'd spoken in my defense, it worried me that the *meloxie* wouldn't look at me or let me say anything about what had happened. "Not now! Tomorrow!" she answered when I tried to speak.

After the *meloxie* left, I lay on my back and stared upward at the ceiling, which was stained with gray streaks and shiny from the constant brewing of beer. I'd never noticed that before—most nights I was so tired my eyes closed the moment I lay down on my pallet. But that night I lay still, my body tense and ready to flee at the first sign of attack. I was too frightened to cry.

After a while, a picture entered my head—the flash of a knife and a soldier's hand lying on the ground, fingers still curling and uncurling. He must have felt pain, for I remembered his screams. Lewteh and I had clung to each other, and after a while the sounds had dwindled to quiet sobbing.

If they cut off my foot, would my toes continue to move? I shut my eyes tight, even though I knew that it wouldn't erase the picture of that hand, or the memory of the head I'd seen lying on the ground in Gondar City, its eyes wide and staring.

Later, I heard the usual noises of the *arakie beit* being shut down for the night. I should pray, I thought. But I didn't feel prayerful. I was filled with fear—and anger, more anger than I'd ever felt in my life. Instead of praying, I ranted at God and cursed the girl from school.

Are you blind? I asked God. Can't you see what's happening? I thought you'd find a way for me to be a free person—not a slave that has to get up in the dark and work until it's dark again. And now look what's happened! Is this what you planned for me—to be maimed and tied up and forced to work until I'm dead?

And that stupid girl, what was she thinking? What right did Hailu have to come here and destroy everything? So—these crazy people say that we Jews have powers? Well, if we do, then I curse that girl and wish her a horrible fate!

A few hours later, I heard loud cries coming from the house next door, and I got up and crept through the dark passage to the edge of the living room. "*Minden now*, what is it?" Yelemwork shouted to the neighbors.

"Aiee! The girl from Semien has been hurt!" Helen called back.

I leaned against the wall, shocked. Had God heard my curse?

I strained to hear the conversation that was going on between the two houses. It seemed that a group of soldiers had been drinking in the *tela beit* next door. An argument had broken out and my former schoolmate had said something that inflamed their tempers. The soldiers dragged her out of the house, took her to a nearby field, and raped her.

Now the girl was wailing so loudly that I could barely make out what she was saying. Then I heard her say, very clearly, "It was the *falasha* that did it! She's the one who brought this down on me, the miserable *kayla*. I told you she was trouble! Didn't I warn you? If you don't do something about her, you'll all die in your beds one day!"

"Yes, you did tell us," Helen answered. "Yelemwork, you'd better be very careful while this creature remains in your house. It would be better to get rid of her as soon as possible!"

The women conferred anxiously, until the *meloxie* said, "It's late, go to bed, everyone. We'll talk about it tomorrow."

Slowly, the women dispersed and the household fell silent.

Chapter 21

Amba Giorgis, February 21, 1992
Wuditu, 16

I lay on my bed trying desperately to think of a way to save myself. Was there anyone I could ask for help? Berreh was a decent man. I considered asking him to hide me in his hotel. But I'd lied to him. If I told him the truth, could I trust him not to turn against me? I was afraid to take a chance.

Well before dawn, I got up to fetch water. I tried to wash away the signs of my weeping. I told myself that I mustn't show any weakness or fear.

All the way, I silenced the voices in my head that were crying, Run! Run while you have a chance! I don't know why I didn't follow that voice. Perhaps I was just too tired of fighting to stay alive. I filled my jugs and trudged back with them, my feet heavy and my heart pounding wildly.

When I returned, Yelemwork said coldly, "Get everything ready for the market. I want to leave early today. We'll speak of those other matters," she sneered, "after we've finished our marketing."

I thought, As long as she needs me to work, I'll be safe. As relieved as I was, I knew that it was only temporary.

I was standing with my baskets and waiting for my mistress when Berreh came running into the courtyard, nose twitching at the smell of freshly brewed coffee. What could he want so early in the day?

"Where's your mistress, Wuditu?" he asked, breathing heavily. I pointed to the interior of the house.

"What's your father's name, sister?" Berreh asked me. He grabbed my arm and held on tightly. I stayed silent, frightened by his painful grip and sharp tone.

"A *faranj* woman was here a few days ago, looking for you. Did you know that?" he asked.

"No," I answered, shocked. I'd heard nothing of this. Who could be asking for me?

"She came back again this morning," he said. "I promised I'd bring you to the kiosk to talk to her."

"I can't come with you. I have to go to the market with my mistress," I protested.

"You're not going to the market today. You're coming with me," he said and continued to hold onto my arm. His other hand rested on the revolver he kept in his belt. I'd gotten so used to seeing him with it that I no longer paid any attention, but now I suddenly felt frightened.

"Berreh, it's Saturday—this girl is coming to market with me," Yelemwork said determinedly.

"Yelemwork, did you know that someone was asking for Wuditu?" the *meloxie* asked angrily, having heard what Berreh said.

"She knew. I told her so myself," Berreh answered for

Yelemwork, when she remained silent.

"That was very wrong of you! Why didn't you say anything about it?" the *meloxie* persisted.

"I didn't think it was important," Yelemwork scoffed. "Anyway, it doesn't matter. I need her to help me with the marketing. She can meet this person another time."

"Nonsense!" the *meloxie* said firmly. "You can go to the market by yourself for once. I don't know what you were thinking, Yelemwork. She ought to at least be allowed to find out why the *faranj* has come. It may be important. Go on—go with Berreh," the *meloxie* said to me, then held up her hand to stop us. "Wait! You can't go like that!" she said. "Here, cover yourself with my *netela*."

As she leaned forward to give me her shawl, she whispered in my ear, "Try to get away, Wuditu! Save yourself!"

She waited to see if I had heard. When she saw that I had, she nodded slightly. Her eyes were troubled but determined. The *meloxie* gave me a push toward Berreh, and he began to pull me by the arm toward the center of town, barely stopping when I stumbled and nearly fell. I threw the *meloxie*'s *netela* over my head and around my shoulders and struggled to keep up the pace.

My head was spinning. Thoughts raced through my mind. Would my father send a woman to look for me? Would he send a *faranj*? I wanted so badly to believe that it could be someone from my family, but it just didn't seem right that a foreign woman would come for me.

A crowd was gathered by the kiosk in the center of town. When Berreh dragged me forward, they all turned to look at me. I didn't see any foreigner there, just the usual crowd of townspeople that gathered to gape on the rare occasion when a *faranj* appeared.

I looked inquiringly at Berreh. "*Tigist*, patience, the *faranj* was here a few minutes ago. She has gone to the north, but she said she'll be back in a little while," he said.

"Wuditu, are you a *falasha*?" a woman in the crowd asked me. I recognized her as someone I'd seen in the queue at the flour mill.

I shook my head vigorously in denial.

"They say that the *faranj* was here once before, with people from Israel," the woman persisted. "What would they want with you, if you're not a *falasha*?"

"I'm not a *falasha*," I insisted. "I'm a Christian. But I'm from Semien and there are a lot of *falashas* living near my parents' village. Maybe they wanted to ask me about someone from there." I thought it was a clever lie, but the woman looked at me with disbelief.

Berreh said nothing all this time but kept a tight grip on my arm.

"The *faranj* promised to pay Berreh if he brought you here," a man said snidely, and Berreh hissed back, "*Unte*, you—mind your own business!"

The constant muttering of the crowd was making me very nervous. I wrapped my head and shoulders in the *meloxie*'s *netela* until only my eyes remained uncovered. I sank down wearily onto a large rock, trying to make myself as small as possible.

"Don't think of trying to run away!" Berreh said. He released my arm but continued to keep a close watch over me.

We waited for what seemed like hours, and I watched

Berreh warily from under lowered eyes. He was being so cold toward me—this was so different from his usual behavior. I thought it must be the money that was causing him to act this way. Who could resist the promise of a reward?

A short time later, Yelemwork arrived. "What's happening? Are you still waiting? Berreh, I need Wuditu's help. Give her to me," she said, grabbing my arm and trying to pull me up. But Berreh refused to let go of me.

"The *faranj* will be back any minute now," Berreh replied. "We're not moving from here until she comes!"

"I heard that the woman has promised to pay you for finding Wuditu," Yelemwork said nastily. "You didn't say anything about that to me! But remember, it was me who fed this girl and gave her a roof over her head. It was me who bought her medicine when she was sick. She belongs to me—don't forget that, Berreh. If that woman gives you any money for this girl, you'd better give me a share, yes?"

Berreh nodded, with his eyes still glued to the entrance to town.

To me, Yelemwork said, "All right. Wait here for the *faranj*, you miserable girl. What's the point of having a servant if I have to carry everything by myself?" With a loud sigh she turned and left me to face the crowd in the square.

Hours later, there was still no sign of the *faranj*. My mouth was dry and, sitting so close to the ground, my eyes were leaking tears from the dust stirred up by people trudging back and forth to market. I felt a hundred eyes on me, all staring suspiciously. I hadn't eaten at all that day or the night before. I felt weak and my stomach gnawed even more painfully than usual. In a few hours it would be dark. What would we do if the woman didn't come back? Were we going to spend the whole night at the kiosk?

It was a long time later when a taxi finally pulled up and stopped beside the kiosk. Berreh and I stood back, watching as the crowd surged around the car and began to riot, yelling, "*Faranj, faranj, faranj*" in high, piercing voices.

Men banged on the car with their fists, trying to get the attention of the *faranj*. "Mother, money, sister, money!" they yelled. Children scrabbled at the taxi, trying to remove its parts. When the driver saw this, he got out of the taxi and waved a thick stick at the crowd.

Berreh pushed forward, dragging me behind him and using his revolver to prod anyone who stood in his way. He opened the back door, shoved me into the car, sat down on the seat beside me, and said, "Here she is! Now where's my money?"

My whole body was trembling. Where to hide? I crouched down on the floor, hid my face in the *netela*, and prayed.

"Get up, girl," a woman's voice said in Amharic. I stole a look upward and saw an old white woman peering down at me from the front seat. There was no kindness in her face. She was struggling to hold on to a rope that was attached to the handle of her door, while the crowd surrounding the car tried to pull it open. She seemed just as frightened as I was. Who was she? Why was she here? What did she want with me? Could this woman have possibly come from my family?

"What's your name?" the foreigner asked me.

I didn't answer.

"Are you a *falasha*?" she asked.

"No!!" I shouted. I lowered my head and stared at my white shrouded knees. I thought, Stupid woman, you'll get us both killed!

Berreh said more firmly, "I've brought you the girl you were looking for. Now give me the money you promised."

Berreh and the *faranj* both began yelling, but I could see that they were having trouble understanding each other. The *faranj* said something to the driver and he began to translate for her and Berreh.

I tried to understand what the driver was saying. I listened so carefully that I must have stopped breathing. All of a sudden, I had trouble catching my breath. I gasped in panic and stopped trying to hear what the three were saying. I struggled to breathe slowly and carefully. After a while, my breathing returned to normal, my heartbeat slowed, and I was able to listen again.

Over the roar of the crowd I heard the *faranj* say, "I'm not sure this is the right girl. You're frightening her and she won't answer my questions."

Berreh turned toward me and shouted, "Answer the *faranj*, girl!"

"Leave her alone," the woman said loudly. "What we need is some quiet. Can you please get out of the car and try to quiet the crowd for a few minutes? I need to finish questioning her and it's impossible to do that with so much noise all around us."

Berreh said, "What about my money?"

"If she's the girl I'm looking for, you'll be paid—you

and everyone who helped you," the *faranj* promised.

When Berreh showed no sign of getting out of the car, the *faranj* insisted, "If you don't give me a chance to question her in peace, you won't get your money."

This *faranj* must be crazy! I thought, terrified. The crowd won't wait for her to give them the money. Look at them! They're attacking the car! They'll simply take it from her by force and she'll die right along with me. *Faranj* or not, the life of a Jew is worth nothing in this town.

I peered at the woman and saw that, despite her brave words, she was trembling. I could smell her fear.

Berreh looked at the crowd and then back at the *faranj*. I waited fearfully. What would he decide to do? To my great relief, he hesitated, nodded, and then got out of the taxi.

When he was gone, the *faranj* turned around in her seat and said in a stern voice, "Now, you will tell me the truth, *falasha* girl!"

Chapter 22

Amba Giorgis, February 21, 1992

Wuditu, 16

I remained silent, crouched on the floor of the car. My knees were aching, but I was too frightened to move. I wanted to help the woman, but I didn't know what to answer. Would it be better to tell her the truth? Or should I make up a lie? If I lied—what kind of a lie would be safer for me?

I'd been trembling uncontrollably all day, but suddenly I realized that the shaking I was feeling wasn't coming from inside my body. I peered upward and I couldn't believe what I was seeing. A group of men and boys were leaning on the car and rocking it from side to side, trying to overturn the taxi! God of Israel, I prayed. Help me! They're trying to kill us!

"Hurry up! Is that her? Is that the girl you're looking for?" the driver shouted at the *faranj*. There was a note of panic in his voice and his eyes were huge. He knew very well what was going to happen to us.

The crowd on my side of the car was pushing and

pushing. The rocking got worse. If nothing stopped it, we would soon be turned on our heads!

One man was trying to open the door on the *faranj*'s side of the car. She was still holding onto the rope that kept her door closed, and now the driver closed his fist over the rope too and helped her to keep it closed. Another man spat on the window right by her face and she cringed. There were shouts of "*Buda! Kayla! Falasha!*" from all around us.

The *faranj* turned around, reached out a hand, and grabbed my chin, forcing my entire body upward. She widened the gap in the *netela* and peered at my face. She seemed disappointed with what she saw

"*Y'abatie, sime man now*—what's your father's name?" the foreigner yelled. I caught sight of Berreh, shooting his revolver in the air outside the car. When the men heard the shots, they fell back and the rocking stopped abruptly.

"Berihun," I whispered. "My father's name is Berihun." If she hadn't been watching my lips she wouldn't have caught the sound over the noise of the crowd. I dropped the *netela* to my shoulders and looked straight at the *faranj* for the first time.

"Who is this?" she shouted, forcing my chin upward so I could see that she had a pile of photographs in her hand.

I took them from her and stared at the one on top. "Lewteh!" I whispered, tears pouring down my cheeks. "Lewteh," I kept saying over and over.

"*Baka*, enough!" the driver yelled. "Hurry up. We've got to get out of here."

"What happened to your father in Sudan?" she asked me.

"I got lost," I answered, mistaking her intent.

"No, what happened to his face?" she insisted.

"He hurt his eyes," I answered. The driver translated what I had said. I saw by her expression that I had given the answer she wanted.

"*Ba'al alesh*, do you have a husband?" she asked.

"No," I answered.

"*Lijoch alesh*, do you have children?"

"No."

The foreigner seemed relieved. She watched me steadily, took a deep breath, and asked, "Will you come with me to Israel? Your parents are waiting for you there."

"When shall I come—when?" I asked fearfully. If she left me here, Yelemwork would punish me, perhaps even kill me.

"Right now! " she answered, and I felt a rush of hope that I might still escape with my life.

"Who will look after me?" I asked.

"I will," she answered. "I'll watch over you until I can bring you to your father. But someone told me that you are a slave. Is that true?" the *faranj* asked me. I nodded, yes.

The woman rolled her window down a little and shouted to Berreh. "This girl is a slave. I can't take her with me. I have to pay for her first," she said, while the driver shouted his translation. "We can't do that here, with all this noise. Please help us turn the taxi around and drive a little way out of town. If you bring her mistress to us, we'll see if she'll sell the girl. If she will, I'll pay you."

"I've already done my part. You must pay me no matter what the woman decides," Berreh insisted, his hand on his revolver.

"Very well, I'll pay you no matter what the girl's mistress says," she said hastily. "But you must help us turn the car around," she repeated when she saw that Berreh was looking first at the crowd and then at the car. He was hesitating, not sure what to do.

Looking outside, I could see why the woman wanted to turn the car around. And I could see why Berreh was hesitating. The front of the car was facing the kiosk. With the crowd surrounding us on all sides, we were trapped. But if he let us turn the car around, we might have a chance to escape. My heart was pounding.

After a moment's thought, Berreh nodded and began to shout at the crowd, promising that money would be handed out if we did as he asked. The crowd parted and slowly, slowly, the driver managed to turn the car around. We drove a few hundred metres in the direction of Gondar City and the crowd walked alongside the car, shouting and jeering at us and waving sticks in the air.

"*Stop!*" Berreh stood in front of the car and held up his hand. "That's far enough!"

Yelemwork appeared suddenly at my window and shouted, "Wuditu, Wuditu!"

"Where is the *meloxie*?" I sobbed, reaching to open the car door.

"Don't you dare open that door!" the *faranj* shouted, and the driver leaned over to press the door lock.

"I have to give the *meloxie* back her *netela*," I tried to explain. "I want to say good-bye and thank her for treating me kindly."

The *faranj* looked at me as though I was crazy. "If you

open that door, I'll leave you here," she replied harshly.

I let my hand drop from the door handle and watched while the *faranj* bargained and then paid for me. Five hundred birr changed hands. Yelemwork was supposed to have paid me for all the work I had done. Now the *faranj* was paying her! It didn't seem right. But I was much too frightened to do anything but watch as the money was handed through a small crack in the car window.

Yelemwork beamed a false smile at me before adding, "Wait a minute! The girl was sick and I bought medicine for her. And that *netela* she's wearing? It belongs to my grandmother. It's not so easy to come by them, you know," she said. "If you want the girl, you'll have to pay for the medicine and the *netela* and the good care that my grandmother and I gave her."

The *faranj* won't be so stupid as to give her more money, I thought in disgust. But, before I could say anything, she had handed another hundred birr through the window. She then turned to me and asked, "Wuditu, do you have any things you want to take with you?"

I looked down at my clothes and spread my arms, saying, "No, I have no things, only these clothes."

Berreh's face appeared at my window. He tried to open the door and when he found it locked he began to shout furiously and bang on the driver's window with the butt of his revolver. The driver, afraid that Berreh would break the window, rolled it down enough to let him speak with the *faranj*. They began to bicker over the money that was owed him, but the crowd, having seen money change hands, started to gather around the car again, rocking it from side to side again, trying to turn it over.

Berreh turned away from the car, trying to regain control over the crowd. But as I watched, he fell and was trampled by the crowd. I heard shots and thought, If Berreh is gone, nothing can save us now! We're going to die!

"Do something!" the *faranj* yelled at the driver. But he was staring helplessly out the window. I watched, terrified, as the crowd continued to rock the car. I looked at the hatred in the eyes of the men outside my window. We were all frozen in place, like a photograph that can never be changed. But I knew that in the next moment or two, the car would turn over.

When the *faranj* saw that the driver wasn't going to move, she started to yank open all the zippered pockets of her jacket. Some scraped open, others caught and stuck fast and she muttered in frustration. The crowd scratched at her window but, ignoring them, she rolled it down a few inches and began to pull wads of birr notes out of her pockets. The driver and I looked on, paralyzed, while she rolled down the window even more and threw all the bills out the window!

Out, out, went handfuls of fifty-birr notes, foreign money, and a fistful of wrapped candies. As she did so, a great gust of wind swept it all away.

The crowd paused in their rocking and watched the money float up and above their heads.

"Caramele! Caramele!" Children scrambled to pick up the candies from the ground. The adults turned as one and began to run after the money that was blowing farther and farther away from the taxi.

"*Go! Go!*" the *faranj* shouted to the driver and finally he was able to move. He gunned the motor and my head jerked backward as we were propelled at a great speed away from the crowd and away from the town. I wept with relief while the woman shouted and shouted. She had a broad grin on her face as she turned around to face me in the back seat.

The driver drove wildly, bouncing us painfully over the narrow, pitted road. The *faranj* leaned over the top of her seat and hugged me, nearly falling over on top of me. She laughed triumphantly. I smiled and leaned back against the seat, exhausted and excited, both at the same time. I was free! We were all alive! It was a miracle!

"Stop the car!" The woman suddenly ordered, and the driver pulled the car over to the side of the road. The woman motioned for me to get out of the car. Now what?

The *faranj* pointed to a camera and asked if she could photograph me with the mountains and the sunset in the background. I nodded and bowed. "When we get to Israel I'll give you the photographs to remember this moment," she promised, and I bowed low, embarrassed when I realized that my bobbing up and down was making it hard for her to focus the camera.

The foreigner mimicked me, bobbing up and down too, and I laughed out loud at her antics. It sounded strange to my ears, and I realized that I had not laughed in a very long time. The camera flashed twice and I winced each time, startled at the sudden explosions of light.

We stood for a moment, admiring the sunset, and then got back into the car. I looked uneasily at the gathering darkness, hoping the *shifta'och* would hold off for the rest of the trip. To distract myself from thoughts of bandits, I continued to shuffle through the photographs. I looked up when the foreigner took them from my hands and put them into an envelope. She presented them to me, saying, "This is the first of many things that will be yours from now on."

I bowed, and the foreigner laughed and shook her finger at me, saying, "You mustn't keep bowing. You'll be an Israeli soon, and in our culture we don't bow. You must learn to keep your head up and your long neck high, like a giraffe."

The driver laughed as he translated for her. "My mother says that I have the neck of a giraffe," I said, remembering her stories about my grandmother, Tarik.

"You see?" she said, nodding. "Your mother knew that one day you'd be in a place where you'd never have to bow again!"

Chapter 23

Gondar City, February 28, 1992

Wuditu and Judie

"Are you ready?" Judie asked. "Hurry up. The car will be here any minute."

"So many things," I said, pointing to the open suitcase.

"*Chigger yelem,* no problem," Judie said. She plopped down onto the suitcase and snapped the lock shut. "Done!" she said and I laughed. Why hadn't I thought of that?

"You look beautiful!" she said, looking me over.

I was wearing a blue-flowered dress that we had bought in the market. On my head and shoulders, I wore a thin scarf with flowers that matched the dress. I'd studied myself in the full-length mirror of the hotel and I thought that I looked very pretty. My face and body were already beginning to fill out and my eyes were sparkling with excitement. We were about to fly to Addis Ababa!

It was only seven days since we'd escaped from the mob in Amba Giorgis, but already I could feel my strength returning. That first night I'd been so tired and hungry that

I could barely keep my eyes open. After a quick meal in Judie's hotel, I'd spent a long time in my first bath. When I came out, the heat and the long day made me stumble with exhaustion.

I could tell from the eager way she'd waited for me to come out of the bathroom that Judie had wanted to sit and talk with me. And there were many things I longed to ask her. But she saw that I could barely stand. She said nothing about the scars on my arms and legs and handed me a jar of cream. When I finished smearing the rich lotion all over myself, she pointed toward the bed.

That first night, I was too tired even to wonder why she had come for me. I could only think that it was a miracle that she had. But when we sat down to eat the next morning, there was finally time for us to talk, using an Amharic-Hebrew dictionary and the little we knew of each other's languages. Sometimes people helped us out with translation. But from the very beginning, we understood so much more than what was actually said.

"I first met Lewteh two years ago, when I was working in Addis Ababa," Judie told me. "She was only 10, but she was all alone. And I was working there by myself, far from my own family. So we were both very lonely. During the time we spent together in Ethiopia, we became very close. When we got to Israel, I continued to spend time with her at Berihun and Melkeh's house, and she often came to my house for weekends and holidays."

Judie looked at me with sorrow in her eyes. "Your father told me more than two years ago that he had paid someone to go to Ethiopia to look for you," she said. "But the man came back without you, telling him, 'Your daughter is dead.'"

"'I'm nearly blind from crying for my lost daughter, Wuditu,' Berihun told me sorrowfully. The family mourned your passing," Judie said, "and I never asked about you after that. But a few months ago, I found Lewteh sitting up on her bed in the middle of the night. She was crying and writing in her notebook. 'Who are you writing to?' I asked. 'I'm writing to my sister Wuditu,' she answered. I tried to think of a way to ask, politely, why she was writing to a person who was dead," Judie said, looking at me with one of her ironic smiles.

"'My sister is not dead,' Lewteh answered firmly. 'That man my father paid never went to look for my sister!' she insisted. 'He is a liar and a thief! If my sister was dead, I would know it. She's alive!'

"It was Letweh who made me decide to go to Ethiopia and look for you," Judie said.

I thought, How strange. I'm the older sister. I set out so long ago to rescue Lewteh. But in the end, it was she who rescued me!

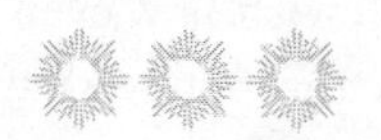

This was a time when I should have been happy and excited, looking forward to rejoining my family and to a better life in Israel. After all, only a short while ago I'd been ill and starving and facing the threat of being maimed or killed.

I was relieved and I did have short bursts of happiness. But I was also depressed and anxious. There were nights when every terrible thing I'd endured came back to me in dreams that left me gasping and frightened and drenched with sweat. I couldn't imagine how I was going to explain my lost years to my family.

When I'd lived in Amba Giorgis, I'd had to lie about being Beta Israel. In Israel, I would have to lie to protect my good name. Will my whole life be filled with lies? I wondered sadly.

I didn't tell anyone how I was feeling, but Judie seemed to understand without my saying anything. She took me aside on my last day in Addis. She thought for a moment and then said, "You do know that whatever was done to you while you were away from your family wasn't your fault, don't you?"

I nodded my head, but in my heart I didn't believe her.

She said, "Your people were separated from the rest of the Jews for a long time, and there are some things about our religious laws that have evolved and changed over the years. When you get to Israel, you'll learn about *piku'ach nefesh*, the saving of human life. We believe that saving a life is more important than anything else, that it overrides almost every other Jewish law, even the one to keep the Sabbath. All the time that you were away from your family, you did everything you could to save your life. Isn't that right?"

"That's true." I nodded, for surviving had been my greatest concern.

"You see—you've fulfilled God's highest law," Judie said. "Not only should you not be blamed for trying to save your life, but according to our laws, you should be praised for doing so."

When I thought about what she said, it did make me feel a little less ashamed, but I still hoped that God would show me the way to save my good name.

I flew to Israel on a bright, sunny afternoon. It was Independence Day, and I was told at the airport that arriving on such a day would bring me good luck. I stared out the window of the taxi on my way to Berihun and Melkeh's apartment in the center of the country.

What I could see of Israel looked nothing at all like Ethiopia. There were no mountains or hills to be seen—it was flat everywhere! The streets were crammed with tall buildings and there was hardly any space between them.

I wondered if it was flat like this all over the country. I hoped not and felt a sudden yearning for towering mountains and the soaring feeling that came over me when I'd climb all the way to the top.

What was I thinking? I'd only just landed—was I already longing for Ethiopia? It didn't make any sense to feel this way!

I lowered my head and twisted my neck and finally I managed to see the top of the tallest building. Perhaps from up there you could see green spaces—possibly even a mountain or two. Was that what people here did when they wanted to be way up above everything else—take an elevator? I laughed at the thought and the driver stared curiously at me in the mirror. What he must think of me, sitting all alone in the back seat and chuckling to myself!

I went back to staring out the window. Everywhere I

looked there were cars lined up, so close they were nearly touching. Horns beeped loudly and there was a strong smell coming from the cars. I covered my nose with my scarf and hoped that where my family lived there would be no such smell. I sat in the taxi and contemplated my first traffic jam.

I'd known that the people around me would all be white, but still it took me by surprise. Here and there, I glimpsed a flash of pale *netela* and a brown face just like mine, someone from my country. But none of them were driving cars. Did my people not know how to drive? I would learn how to do so, that was for sure.

My family didn't know what day I was supposed to arrive. But I was told that because of the holiday they were all gathered together in my father and stepmother's apartment. I climbed the stairs with my suitcase in my hand, my eyes searching the doors for the number 39.

I knocked quietly on the wooden door. I was trembling—happy and terrified all at the same time. My hands were sweaty and I wiped them on my dress, not wanting to touch my family with such a clear sign of fear. When no one answered, I knocked again, louder.

The door swung open. At first, I didn't recognize the elderly woman who stood there. She didn't know me either and it was only after a minute or two that we were able, finally, to move toward each other.

I clung to my mother and we sobbed and sobbed, while people murmured quietly in the background. Her shoulders shook as she cried, and for the first time I thought about the pain my absence must have cost her.

"I'm so sorry, Enutie," I whispered in her ear.

"You have nothing to be sorry for," she answered. Her face was much more lined than I remembered and it was wet with tears. But her smile was just as warm and beautiful as ever. "We're the ones who should be sorry," she said firmly.

I felt an arm around my shoulders, turning me, and there was my brother, Dawid. "Forgive me," he wept.

"*Ishi*, it's okay," I assured him, and he could see in my eyes that I was feeling no anger toward the family. My stepmother kissed my cheeks, asking, too, for forgiveness. "I couldn't find you," she kept saying. "I looked everywhere."

"It wasn't you, Melkeh, it was the soldiers," I told her and she smiled at me with tear-drenched eyes.

My stepsisters gathered around me, hugging and kissing me and murmuring words of praise to God. But Lewteh hung back a little. I moved toward her and we fell into each other's arms, weeping and laughing all at the same time. After a while, I stood back to look at her. She'd been a pretty child, but now she was truly beautiful. And how she was dressed! I'd never even dreamed of such lovely clothes as she was wearing. And her hair—it was dyed bright red! I laughed to see it and she giggled. This was the Lewteh that I remembered! And best of all, her back was as straight as mine.

"*Dehananesh*, are you well?" I asked anxiously.

"I am well," she answered with a smile.

"You saved my life," I said to her, overwhelmed by how brave and how wise my little sister had been.

"If you were dead, I would have known it," Lewteh answered, tears streaming down her cheeks. "I could still feel you breathing, Wuditu," she said with one of her brilliant smiles.

The crowd soon parted, and I saw my father sitting in a chair, waiting for me to come to him. He was old and frail. His eyes were red from weeping and his hands shook.

"Abatie, Father," I cried and ran to him. I knelt down and kissed his hands. I pressed my face against his legs and closed my eyes while he stroked my hair. I could feel his whole body trembling, and when I looked up at him I thought sadly, He is dying.

Neighbors crowded into the apartment until none of us could move. Someone began playing a *masenqo*, and everywhere people were exclaiming and praising God for my miraculous return.

As more and more people crowded around us, all I could think was, In such a crowd, there will be no time for questions. But the opposite was true, and I was mortified when the first questions came from complete strangers.

"Where were you all that time?" an old woman, a neighbor, demanded.

"I worked as a servant, taking care of the children and doing all the housework," I answered. "The head of the household was a very religious woman, a *meloxie*, and she was very good to me."

The visitors muttered approvingly.

"How did you get away from there?" someone else asked, and I told the story of the taxi and the *faranj* who had come for me from so far away.

"A miracle," people kept saying and, miraculously for me, that was the end of the questioning.

There were solemn nods on all sides, and I stood tall like a giraffe, remembering both my mother's and Judie's advice, never to bow my head again.

Epilogue

Jerusalem, Israel, 1997
Wuditu, 21

My birth mother says that I was born twice—once to her and once to Judie. My two mothers have shared my time in the years since I left Ethiopia. And so, every year we all celebrate my two birthdays, the one in December when I was born to Rahel and the one in February that Judie and I call our anniversary.

When I think back to that day, I remember that even in my happiest moments there was a part of me that was worried about whether I could hide my secrets for an entire lifetime. I thought I'd been clever when I implied that I'd spent all of my lost time in the *meloxie*'s house. No one ever asked me anything else about those years because the story of my dramatic rescue caused so much interest. From then on, that's all that people wanted to hear about—how I was freed, not what I had suffered up to that moment. And at first I was happy because I believed that I had saved my good name.

But it wasn't so easy for me to escape my past. Very soon after I arrived, it began to cause me great pain. Sometimes, in the middle of a busy and happy day, I'd have a flash of fear, thinking that I was still trapped in Amba Giorgis.

I've learned that when this happens I must take deep breaths and look around me—at the beautiful clothes I now wear, at the modern city where I now live, and at the two loving families that now surround me—my own large and growing birth family and my adopted family, comprised of Judie and my new brothers.

During the first few months after I arrived, I was preoccupied with learning the language and carrying on with my education. Having lived in such a remote part of Ethiopia, I knew nothing about almost everything—including world history. Learning that other Jewish communities had suffered losses as great if not greater than mine was an eye-opener.

At first I found myself turning away wherever there was a news broadcast about Darfur or about other violent African conflicts. They reminded me too much of what I'd been through. But after a while I began to watch, and I started to think about writing my story and having it read by others. I thought it might help me to rid myself of all that pain. But I also thought that if people read about my life as a captive, it might help people to understand the lives of other children living as slaves—not only in Ethiopia but all over the world.

I did worry about what my people would think of me when they read my story. Would they judge me harshly? Or would they see me the way Judie's family does—as a hero?

I hope that when the time comes, I'll have the courage

to stand proudly before my people, knowing that at every stage I chose a path that led to survival and a return to my family.

Sometimes, I still wake up shaking and scared. I still have regrets and some of my memories still fill me with shame. But I have also come to be proud of the path I walked.

And sometimes, when I'm with my relatives, I still put my hands together and bow before my elders. But I no longer have even the slightest inclination to bow down before anyone else. And I've learned to take great pride in the long neck that is so prized by the *faranj*. After all, it's always good to have an advantage in life, especially one that is bequeathed to you by your ancestors.

Glossary

Abatie = Father

aizosh = be brave, you are brave

Amlak Israel = God of Israel

ankalba = pouch for carrying babies

arakie = home-made beer

arakie beit = beer hall

baka! = enough!

berbere = hot red peppers, used to make a sauce

Beta Israel = House of Israel, the Ethiopian Jews' name for themselves

birr = Ethiopian currency

birtukan = an orange, the colour orange

buda = derogatory term for a Jew, a person who possesses the evil eye

buna = local coffee

chakla = child

chigger yelem = it's no problem, or that's okay

dehananeh, dehananesh = are you well, for a male, and for a female

Enutie = Mother

falasha = a negative term for a Jew

faranj = a foreigner, a white person

Fasika = Passover

Gondar Province, Gondar City = a province and the provincial capital, in Northern Ethiopia

injera = flat, sourdough bread, fermented for several days, causing a sour taste

ishi = okay, it's all right

kabele = the local administration

kayla = negative term for a Jew, meaning hyena

kemis = cotton dress

kes, kesoch = religious leader(s)

ketab = talisman worn to ward off evil spirits

kitta = unleavened bread made for Passover

kwayu = be still

lij, lijoch = child, children

masenqo = a single-stringed violin

meloxie = a person who has lived a normal life and then become religious, a nun

mergem gojo = menstrual hut, where women stay for seven days during their menstruation and after childbirth

merkato = market

mesgid = synagogue

mgogo = flat, round frying pan, made by the Jews from local clay for use and for sale

minden now? = what is it?

netela = white head and body covering, sometimes with embroidered bands at the ends

shifta, shifta'och = bandit(s)

Sigd = a holiday unique to the Beta Israel

tef = special iron-rich grain that grows only in Ethiopia

tela = home-made beer

tela beit = beer hall

tenastelign = good day

tigist = patience

Timkat = Easter

unchee = you, for a female

unte = you, for a male

wot = a sauce to eat on injera bread, made of spices and meat, vegetables, legumes, fish, or chicken

wotader, wotader'och = soldier(s)

Yerusalem = the name the Beta Israel called the Land of Israel

Yxaviher = God

zabanya = servant

Acknowledgments

Cry of the Giraffe was written out of love and admiration for a daughter who bravely endured a lengthy and brutal captivity yet emerged a generous and caring human being.

What was originally meant to be a memoir evolved instead into a story closely based upon Wuditu's experiences. In order to protect her privacy, some names and events have been altered. I send my love and kudos to Lewteh, who at a young age shared some of her sister's terrifying experiences and then quite a few of her own.

My deep love and respect goes out to my sons, Daniel and Jonathan, who helped to absorb two lost girls into our family and who showed remarkable tolerance for the mother who believed that this would be a good thing for all of us.

Many people have patiently educated me about the Beta Israel community over the last quarter-century. In particular, I would like to thank Susan and Zimna Berhani, Yeshayahu Chane, and Batia Avni, who have struggled in their roles as *astamari'och* (teachers). Yoni, Ruth, Rosemary, Lori, Michal, and Henry—your critical input and support were invaluable.

I am grateful to Barbara Berson for her heroic editing efforts and to all the team at Annick Press for their support and encouragement.

I would like to thank the Ontario Arts Council for their support of this project.